CHEERLEADERS

DATING

CHEERLEADERS

Trying Out
Getting Even
Rumors
Feuding
All the Way
Splitting
Flirting
Forgetting
Playing Games
Betrayed
Cheating
Staying Together
Hurting
Living It Up
Waiting
In Love!
Taking Risks
Looking Good
Making It
Starting Over
Pulling Together
Rivals
Proving It
Going Strong

Stealing Secrets
Taking Over
Spring Fever
Scheming
Falling in Love
Saying Yes
Showing Off
Together Again
Saying No
Coming Back
Moving Up
Changing Loves
Acting Up
Talking Back
All or Nothing
Getting Serious
Having It All
Fighting Back
Telling Lies
Pretending
Here to Stay
Overboard!
Dating

CHEERLEADERS

#47

DATING

JUDITH WEBER

SCHOLASTIC INC.
New York Toronto London Auckland Sydney

ISBN 0-590-41918-8

12 11 10 9 8 7 6 5 4 3 2 1   8 9/8 0 1 2 3/9

Printed in the U.S.A.   01

First Scholastic printing, November 1988

For my sister-in-law, Ethel, with love.

CHAPTER

The crowd was going wild. The Tarenton High varsity basketball team was beating St. Cloud High School by six points, and it wasn't even halftime yet. Every shot by Ray Elliot, Tarenton's star center, found its way into the basket with ease.

Mary Ellen Tilford, the new cheerleading coach at Tarenton, jumped up and shouted exuberantly to her cheerleaders, "Cheer for Ray!"

One by one, the team lined up to perform the spelling cheer for the basketball center. Olivia Evans, the captain, tossed the red-and-white pompons to Jessica Bennett, Sean Dubrow, Tara Armstrong, Peter Rayman, and Melissa Brezneski as they took their positions.

Olivia looked up at the Tarenton bleachers, and instantly her eyes met Duffy's. It was as though a magnet drew them together. He smiled and waved as she forced her concentration back to the cheerleading squad. Tonight she was sure that David Douglas Duffy was her first love, but when Walt Manners was in town, and she was with him, Olivia became uncertain. Fortunately, Walt was in New York visiting his parents this weekend, and she could focus on Duffy.

Olivia signaled the squad to kneel in a single line with their fluffy red-and-white pompons held behind them. As she chanted the cheer, she jumped into the air and did a high tally-ho jump with her arms rotating in a wheel motion.

"Give me an 'R'!" she shouted in a strong, clear voice.

An exuberant, roaring "R" filled the auditorium as the students repeated Olivia's call.

"Give me an 'A'!" Jessica shouted as she did a perfect herkie leap with one leg straight and the other bent. Jessica swung both arms out and shook her pompons furiously. As she moved, her long brown hair rippled down her back.

The audience responded with an "A."

Sean signaled to Tara. "Give me a 'Y'!" He jumped into the air, with his pompons tucked tightly against his chest, and did a front somersault. Then Sean landed in a rounded, kneeling position just as Tara started running toward him. She leaped over Sean and slid gracefully into a split while shaking her pompons over her head.

A rousing cheer came from the spectators. Melissa and Peter performed identical split leaps and shouted, "Elliot . . . Elliot . . . can't be beat!"

Mary Ellen looked at the cheerleaders

proudly. Only last year she had worn the short red-and-white pleated skirt and varsity sweater, as captain of the cheerleaders. It had been a perfect senior year. Now she was married to Pres Tilford, and a miracle happened. Coach Ardith Engborg had moved to California, and she, Mary Ellen Kirkwood Tilford, was hired as the new Tarenton cheerleading coach.

The cheer was performed with perfection. Mary Ellen felt a wave of pride. But there was one thing that was wrong with the perfect picture. The basketball team was winning, and the cheerleaders were doing a fabulous job, but Hope was missing.

Olivia walked over to Mary Ellen after the cheer for Ray. "Have you heard from Hope?" she asked anxiously.

Mary Ellen shook her head.

"It's not like her," Olivia replied. "She's never missed a game."

"I'll call her house again," Mary Ellen said. She tried to reassure Olivia with a pat on the shoulder. "I'm sure there's a simple explanation. Perhaps her car broke down on the way to the game."

"Hope would call," Olivia said.

Mary Ellen knew the cheerleading captain was right. Hope would definitely call. For a moment she thought about when she and Tara were kidnapped only a short time ago. No, Mary Ellen thought, it couldn't happen again to another cheerleader.

Mary Ellen glanced up at the big clock protected by the wire cage. Only fifteen minutes

3

had passed, but it seemed like hours. I have to concentrate on the game, she thought.

"Let's do a clapping cheer next," Mary Ellen told Olivia. "The cheerleaders look good tonight. I'm proud of them."

Olivia smiled. She was proud, too. The cheerleaders had had their ups and downs over the past season, but tonight everything was coming together. But she was still worried about Hope Chang. Hope was serious about her schoolwork, serious about her violin, and serious about cheerleading. She'd never miss a game, Olivia said to herself. Something's wrong. Very wrong.

Sean took center stage just as time was called. His eyes searched the crowd for Kate Harmon. He found her surrounded by her friends from St. Cloud High. With her round wire glasses, unruly hair, and oversized St. Cloud sweatshirt, Kate was easy to spot. Sean was thrilled that Tarenton was winning. Having a girlfriend attending a rival team's school could be sticky, he thought. But the two of them had managed to keep their school rivalry from interfering with their relationship.

Sean picked up the megaphone and announced the clapping cheer. But he couldn't resist the temptation to show off a little. After he put the megaphone down he performed a one-armed walkover, then took the classic cheerleader pose with clenched hands on hips. "Ready, let's go!"

"Get that ball. . . ." The audience clapped along with the cheerleaders.

"Raise that score. . . ." Again, everyone clapped.

The other cheerleaders joined the cheer with jumps and claps.

Tara's enthusiasm was bubbling over. Her red hair was bouncing with every movement, making her look as though she were about to fly. From the first row, Patrick Henley was watching every move she made. The emerald engagement ring he gave her sparkled on her finger. Love is great, Tara thought. It makes every minute of every day special.

Tara studied the strong, dark, young man staring at her. He had the quiet strength of a young Clint Eastwood, and the sensitive looks of Rob Lowe. She thought about Tabitha, the little orange kitten Patrick had given her, and she felt warm inside.

Patrick watched the cheerleaders perform. He clapped and smiled, but he felt he was beginning to outgrow the high school scene. His thoughts were filled with his growing moving business and his future plans with Tara. Now that he owned property at Branchwood Lake, and he and Tara were to be married, he felt that he was becoming a responsible adult.

Tarenton had the ball again. Bill Hadley made the basket, and Peter Rayman realized that the basketball team was leading by sixteen points.

"We're blowing them away!" Peter said enthusiastically to Melissa as they watched the game.

"The team looks great. Bill isn't even making personal fouls tonight," Melissa said, looking up at the tall, sandy-haired boy with the all-American smile.

Peter was surprised by Melissa's comment. "You're really into the game!"

"Of course! Just because I'm an alternate doesn't mean I'm not following the game!" Melissa said defensively.

"I'm sorry," Peter said sheepishly. Then he thought, I just don't seem to be able to say the right thing to girls. I haven't had a real relationship with anyone since Hope.

Suddenly he was jolted back into reality. Hope was missing! Peter walked over to Mary Ellen, who was sitting on the bench. She looked beautiful. Peter had had a crush on her when he was a sophomore and she was a cheerleader herself. He wasn't surprised when she took off for New York and a modeling career, but he did not expect her to return to Tarenton so quickly.

"Did you hear from Hope?" he asked Mary Ellen.

"No, Peter. I'll call at halftime," Mary Ellen said. "Oh, Peter, would you please ask Diana to come talk to me? I want to ask her to pull the mascot out of the girls' locker room."

Peter frowned.

Mary Ellen laughed. "I'm not asking her to cheer! Diana's in charge of The Boss, and we can use him at halftime."

"Okay, Mary Ellen, you call the shots. But don't be surprised if she hides inside the mascot

6

and jumps out to perform cheers during the half-time routine."

"Very funny, Peter. Now go tell her that I'd like to speak to her."

Peter walked toward the stunning blonde with the permed hair and colorful butterfly clip. Diana Tucker was in the third row between Richie Morrison and Chris Hunter. Peter hated to admit it, but she looked fabulous in her light-blue turtleneck sweater and faded denim jacket. She was absorbed in conversation with both boys, and didn't notice Peter until he bent over Richie.

"Diana!" Peter called.

She looked up, and her smiled brightened.

"The coach wants to speak to you," Peter said.

She turned to Christopher. "I told you," she said. "The cheerleaders need me."

Peter didn't want to get into a hassle with Diana, so he turned away and leaped down the three steps to rejoin the cheerleaders.

Diana decided not to hurry. She wanted to savor the moment.

"Hope is missing, and the coach probably wants me," Diana said to her companions.

"Diana, isn't Melissa the alternate?" Richie asked. He had taken photographs of the cheer-leaders and knew a little bit about their problems.

"Yes, but I'm a better gymnast than she is. I should have been the alternate, but there was a lot of jealousy. Next year things will be different," Diana said confidently. "All the girls will be graduating except for Hope and Melissa."

Diana ignored Richie and smiled sweetly at Christopher. "Excuse me, but Mary Ellen wants me and I have to go!"

Diana walked slowly down the steps and over to the cheerleaders' bench. Her tight miniskirt made her long legs look endless. Chris was watching her, and she felt as though every eye in the gym were on her. She loved it!

The cheerleaders were preparing to lead the crowd in a school song when Diana approached Mary Ellen.

"You wanted me, Mary Ellen?" Diana asked brightly.

"Yes, Diana. Could you please pull the mascot out of the girls' locker room and help set him up for the halftime cheers?" Mary Ellen said.

For a second, Diana's face dropped, but then she froze it back into her plastic smile. "Of course, Mary Ellen. I'd do anything to help the cheerleaders."

Ray Elliot made an impossible shot from half court. The crowd started screaming and jumping up and down. The cheerleaders repeated the spelling cheer for Ray, but this time it was twice as loud.

Diana's path to the locker room was filled with cheering fans. She pushed her way through as she tried to block out the resounding cheers, and was relieved when the heavy metal locker-room door clanged shut behind her. She felt alone and angry as she went to retrieve the mascot.

The Boss was over six feet tall and was kept in the storage closet. Diana pulled the mascot out of the closet just as the phone began to ring.

"Shoot!" She looked at the phone on the desk in Mary Ellen's office. "Who could be calling?"

Diana dashed across the room to the office, and grabbed the phone.

"Hello," she said breathlessly.

"Hello, is Mary Ellen there?"

"She's at the game. Who's this?" Diana asked, even though she was certain she recognized the voice.

"Hope Chang . . . I have to get a message to Mary Ellen." Hope paused. "Is that you, Diana?"

"What's the message?" Diana asked, ignoring the question.

"I'm at the emergency room at Tarenton General Hospital," she said quickly.

"What happened?" Diana questioned.

"I can't explain because I'm in a pay booth, but I can't make the game tonight. Will you *please* tell Mary Ellen?" Hope asked anxiously.

"Sure, Hope," Diana said sweetly.

"Thanks," Hope answered and quickly hung up without giving Diana a chance to ask more questions.

Diana put down the phone. Why is she at the hospital? Diana wondered as she walked slowly back to the closet that held the mascot. As she carefully took it out and balanced The Boss on its platform, she thought about her conversation with Hope. Hope doesn't know who answered the phone. She only guessed that it was me. Should I give Mary Ellen the message or forget it? If Mary Ellen thinks that Hope isn't responsible about calling, maybe she'll ask her to leave the squad and then there would be room for a new alternate!

Diana struggled with the door and the mascot.

"Need help?" Christopher shouted from the stands.

Diana formed a coquettish smile.

"I'll be right down," Christopher said as he raced down two steps and vaulted over the railing.

"Don't let me ever see you do that again, young man," a teacher said as Christopher pushed through the crowd to get to Diana.

She batted her eyelashes at him and said, "I don't want you to get in trouble because of me."

"No sweat," Christopher replied. "How about a Coke after the game?"

"Sure. There will probably be a victory party at the Pizza Palace," Diana said as she glanced at the scoreboard and saw Tarenton's substantial lead. "I'd love to go, Chris."

"Over here," Mary Ellen shouted above the roaring cheers from the crowd.

Christopher pulled the wolf's platform as Diana steadied the oversized mascot.

Ray Elliot sunk another basket, and the crowd cheered wildly. The cheerleaders ignored Diana, Christopher, and the mascot.

Finally Mary Ellen returned her attention to

Diana. "We'll use him at halftime," she shouted over the noise. "Thanks for getting him," Mary Ellen said as she took over maneuvering The Boss.

Diana turned abruptly and grabbed Christopher's arm. "Let's get out of here now," she said angrily.

Mary Ellen didn't notice Diana leaving the gym. Her concern was Hope. She called to Olivia. "I'm going to call the Chang house again. Maybe Hope's home now. Set up for halftime, Olivia."

The captain nodded, then helped pull the mascot to the center of the sideline. "I'm worried about Hope, too," she said to Peter and Tara.

The halftime buzzer sent the crowd into another frenzy of cheering. The Tarenton Wolves were beating St. Cloud by twenty-two points. It was the biggest halftime lead the basketball team had had this season, and the crowd wanted the team to know that they appreciated them!

The six cheerleaders moved into the center of the court and started their halftime performance without Hope.

CHAPTER

During halftime, Mary Ellen dashed into her office to call Hope Chang's house. The moment she entered the small office she felt something was wrong. The telephone was facing away from the chair and a pile of papers was askew. She checked her drawers expecting to find something missing, but everything was in place.

Mary Ellen took out her address book and quickly looked up Hope's telephone number. Although everything she did was automatic, she felt uncomfortable, almost like another presence was there in the room. Carefully, she unlocked the phone. Anyone could answer the phone, but the lock controlled outgoing calls.

She dialed and listened impatiently as the phone rang and rang at Hope's house. After a dozen rings, Mary Ellen put down the receiver and relocked the phone.

There's something going on, she thought, as

she returned to the excitement of the basketball game.

The Tarenton Wolves beat St. Cloud by a wide margin of thirty-four points. The spectators were yelling and cheering hysterically. It had been weeks since the Wolves had won a game, and the students could not control their enthusiasm for their team.

The voice of Mrs. Oetjen, the principal, boomed over the loudspeaker. "Congratulations, Wolves! You did a fine job. Now students, walk slowly, and leave the gymnasium in an orderly fashion, without pushing. Thank you."

Mary Ellen immediately told the cheerleaders to form a line. "If we can get the crowd involved in a group cheer, perhaps they'll calm down," she told Olivia.

"Good idea," Olivia replied as she picked up the megaphone and signaled to the cheerleaders to do the same.

"Victory cheer!" The captain shouted.

Mary Ellen stood on the side and called to the six cheerleaders. "Get their attention with some jumps and cartwheels."

Sean and Peter did several spectacular leaps while Tara, Jessica, and Melissa did cartwheels. Olivia started the cheer.

"V-I-C-T-O-R-Y! What do we have?
VICTORY . . . VICTORY . . .
VICTORY!"

Everyone joined in and shouted the word "victory" over and over again. This single word rang out throughout the gym and vibrated from the walls and ceiling.

The pushing stopped, and the crowd put its excitement into cheering.

The cheerleaders continued.

"VICTORY . . . VICTORY . . . VICTORY!"

Mary Ellen was relieved when she saw the crowd leaving the gymnasium in an orderly fashion. Without realizing it, she had also mentally passed from being a student to being part of the faculty. A year ago, she would never have been concerned with crowd control.

The basketball teams had gone into the locker rooms to shower, and a few St. Cloud supporters were sitting alone near the door to the visiting team's dressing room.

Kate broke away from her friends and walked calmly to the bench where the cheerleaders were picking up their equipment before going to the showers.

"Congratulations, Sean," Kate said coolly. "You deserved a win, but I'm sorry it was at my school's expense."

"It was a great game," Sean said cheerfully, ignoring her lack of enthusiasm. He leaned over and pulled her sweatshirt playfully. "When are you going to wear *my* sweatshirt?"

"Don't hold your breath!" she teased as she stepped back and pushed up her glasses.

Sean loved their bantering. He bent down and

whispered, "How about taking the long drive home around the lake?"

"Sean, I'm hungry."

"For me, I hope," he answered conceitedly. Sean's dark good looks and suave manner made him popular with the girls. Since his mother died, he had lived the bachelor life with his father, and he had picked up his father's easygoing attitude toward life.

"Pizza will do," Kate said quickly.

Patrick suddenly appeared in between them. "Did I hear the word 'pizza'?"

"Yes, you did, Patrick," Kate said. "Although Sean doesn't seem to understand the meaning of 'I'm hungry.' "

"Then drop him, old girl, and come to the Pizza Palace with Tara and me. We're not prejudiced against St. Cloud natives."

"You're on," Kate said, winking at Patrick.

"Okay . . . okay," Sean said. "It's pizza first. *Then* I'll drive you home."

"We'll see," Kate answered.

"Look, I've got to shower and change. Tara and I will meet you guys out front."

Sean darted toward the boys' locker room, turned around once to wave to Kate, and disappeared into the room.

In the girls' locker room, Melissa and Jessica were showering, while Tara was drying her long red hair. Mary Ellen, still in her red-and-white sweatsuit, was talking to Olivia in her office.

Olivia pulled her heavy cheerleading sweater over her head and wiped the back of her neck with a towel. "What an exciting game," she said enthusiastically.

"Yes, it was great winning," Mary Ellen said as she closed the door behind Olivia. She admired the captain of the cheerleaders. Olivia Evans had overcome a physical problem and an overprotective mother. She had become not only a strong gymnast, but a highly competent leader of the squad.

"I've been phoning Hope's house but no one is home," Mary Ellen said as she sat on the edge of her desk.

"Hope said her parents were going to be away for the week. I think her father was speaking at a medical convention," Olivia said. "Her brother, James, must be out also."

Mary Ellen nodded thoughtfully. "There's something else."

Olivia frowned. She could tell from Mary Ellen's voice that the coach was troubled.

Mary Ellen pointed to the phone. "Someone used my phone during the first half. Do you have any idea who it could be?"

Olivia shrugged her shoulders. "The cheerleaders were outside during the first half. None of us left the gymnasium." She paused. "But, Mary Ellen, didn't you send Diana in here to get the mascot?"

"You're right. But she didn't say anything about a phone call," Mary Ellen said. After a long hesitation, she said, "If Hope called and Diana answered, do you think she'd avoid giving me the message?"

"I wouldn't put it past her!" Olivia said.

Mary Ellen took a deep breath. "First things first. I have to find Hope. . . . I think I'll drive over to her house and check things out."

"I'll go with you," Olivia offered.

"Don't you have a date with Duffy?" Mary Ellen asked.

"Sure. But Duffy's a reporter. He loves a good story, and Hope's disappearance is one. In fact, I think I'll tell the team what our plans are. I'm sure some of the others will want to check on the Chang home, too."

"I don't know," Mary Ellen said. "I don't want to create a scene."

Olivia answered firmly. "We're all worried about Hope, and you might need us if she's in trouble."

"I guess you're right," Mary Ellen conceded.

Olivia announced the plan to the other girls.

"Count me in," Jessica said quickly.

Tara looked up from drying her hair. "Listen, I've got a date with Patrick. I'm worried about Hope, too, but I hardly have time to see Patrick during the week, because of his moving business and my cheerleading practice. Besides, you'll be there with Mary Ellen and Pres."

"Pres isn't coming. He's at a dinner party at his parents' house," Mary Ellen said as she walked into the room. "But the truth is, we don't need everyone, Tara. So enjoy your date."

"I can't go, either," Melissa said. "I told my parents I'd be home right after the game to baby-sit. My father's picking me up. Will you call me when you hear something?"

17

"Of course, Melissa," Mary Ellen assured her. "I'm going to tell Sean and Peter our plans now."

The parking lot was practically empty when Jessica and Peter got into Mary Ellen's car. Peter sat in the backseat. When Mary Ellen started the engine, Peter began a conversation with an imaginary date. "Come a little closer, gorgeous, I'll keep you warm. Snuggle right up against me!"

"Peter! What's going on?" Jessica exclaimed, turning her head toward the backseat.

Peter had an arm around his "date." "I'm keeping her warm."

"You're nuts, Peter Rayman," Jessica said.

"No, desperate. I haven't had a serious relationship since I broke up with Hope."

"You broke up with Hope? I thought it was the other way around," Jessica said.

"What difference does it make?" Peter said. "Over is over."

"Well, Peter, you seem to have developed a mature philosophy about love," Mary Ellen said as she drove down Main Street.

"What I've developed is the realization that I need a girlfriend."

Jessica started to laugh. "You have lots of girls following you around. Take your pick, Peter."

Peter sank deep into the backseat. "I'm bored with dating. I want a relationship."

"Take it from me," Jessica said seriously, "relationships can be painful. You're better off just dating."

18

Mary Ellen turned to Jessica. "Your feelings will change again, Jessica."

"Right now, I'd rather not have feelings. I'd settle for plain, old dating without complications," Jessica said.

Mary Ellen smiled. She thought about her senior year at Tarenton High. It had been an exciting, confusing time. Now, she and Pres were happy and in love. But, she had to admit she felt like the mother hen of the cheerleaders, and she was only one year older than most of them.

Mary Ellen pulled up in front of the Chang house. She could see in the rearview mirror the headlights of Duffy's car, which had been right behind them.

Peter jumped out of the car. "I'll ring the doorbell. Maybe someone is home watching TV." He zipped up his leather jacket, and dashed up the path.

Jessica turned on the radio and found her favorite rock station. Mary Ellen heard tapping on the driver's window. It was Duffy. She rolled down the window.

"Have room for two more?" he asked.

"Climb in the backseat," Mary Ellen said.

Peter soon reappeared. "No one answered," he said quickly. "Move over," he commanded Olivia and Duffy. "It's cold out here."

The latest song by U2 filled the silence in the car. Mary Ellen kept looking at her watch every few minutes.

"What do you think, Mary Ellen?" Jessica asked finally.

"I just don't know. Maybe we should call the police," Mary Ellen said nervously. She felt it was her responsibility to make the decision. Hope was a member of her team, and she was the coach.

"What about calling the hospital?" Olivia cuddled close to Duffy as she spoke.

"No. Let's not think the worst," Jessica said quickly. "I hate hospitals, and I don't want to even think about Hope being in one."

"Don't be silly. If Hope's in trouble, she may need us. We just can't rule out an accident or illness," Olivia replied.

"Girls," Mary Ellen said, "calm down." She looked at her watch again. "If Hope doesn't show up by eleven o'clock, I think we should check with the police *and* the hospital."

The silence hung heavily in the car. Duffy put his arms around Olivia. Jessica leaned against the car door and closed her eyes, feigning sleep, while Peter drummed his fingers to the beat of the music. Mary Ellen tilted her head back against the headrest. She thought about Pres's car accident, and the nightmare of his recovery when he had to learn to walk again. Perhaps something even worse had happened to Hope, Mary Ellen thought, as she stared into the darkness.

The music was loud and upbeat.

Jessica played with the tuner. "This song is making me nervous." She found a country-music station. Willie Nelson was singing a slow, sad ballad.

Mary Ellen looked again at her watch. "In

five minutes I'm contacting the police. Olivia and Duffy can stay here in case Hope shows up, while we go to the drugstore to call."

Jessica sat up. "Hey, I see headlights. It could be Hope."

Peter leaned forward. "Other people live on this street, too."

"I know," Jessica snapped. "But it looks like the car is slowing down."

The car turned into the Chang driveway and stopped. Peter let out a loud, "All right!"

Mary Ellen quickly turned on her headlights. "Thank goodness," she said as she recognized Hope in the light.

Quickly, the cheerleaders jumped out of the car and started toward Hope's car.

"Hi," Hope said. "Mary Ellen? Jessica?"

"What happened to you?" Mary Ellen was the first to ask.

Everyone quickly surrounded Hope. She looked confused and a little embarrassed.

"Didn't you get my message?" she asked Mary Ellen.

Mary Ellen shook her head. "I've been very worried, Hope. We never got a message. Who did you give it to?"

"It sounded like Diana, but she didn't give her name," Hope replied. "I told the girl that I couldn't make the game because I was at the hospital."

"Are you okay?" Olivia asked anxiously.

"I'm all right. It's James." She walked around to the other side of the car and opened the door. Hope's brother was sitting with his left arm in a sling. Hope leaned over and unbuckled the safety belt for him.

"I fell," James said.

"I was going to take him to the game tonight," Hope started to explain as she helped her brother out of the car. "My parents are at a medical convention in Chicago, so I thought it would be fun for James to watch me cheer. Anyway, he decided to try one of my leaps and he landed on his arm."

"It looks so easy when Hope does it," James said.

"That's because I've been practicing for years." Hope gave James a gentle push. "March, buddy, it's time for bed." Then she turned to her friends. "Come on in. My mother stuffed the refrigerator. Let's raid it."

"Sounds great to me," Peter said.

Everyone followed Hope and James into the house.

"I'm upset about the mix-up with the message," Hope said as she gave her friends hangers for their coats.

"It sounds like a typical Diana stunt," Olivia said.

"I could kill that girl," Jessica added. "She has caused me so much trouble over the last year."

"She's caused *everyone* trouble," Mary Ellen said. "I've been trying to put the pieces together. I sent Diana to the locker room to get the mascot before halftime."

"That's about when I called. I took James right to the emergency room. I expected to call as soon as we got there, but they took him directly into X ray. I couldn't get to a phone until after the game started."

Hope helped James take off his jacket. "It's not broken!" He held his arm up.

"He's lucky this time," Hope said. "Now go upstairs. I want to spend some time with my friends."

As soon as James was gone, Hope turned her attention to the others. Peter stayed in the background. Being in the Chang house reminded him of when he and Hope had dated. It seemed like years ago, but it was only last fall.

Hope invited everyone into her large, cheerful kitchen. It took only a few minutes to unload the contents of the refrigerator onto the counter. "Let's make hero sandwiches and then take them into the family room."

"Sounds good," Duffy said. "Where's your tape deck, Hope? I've got a tape by a new group I heard at the radio station. I want to get everyone's opinion."

"In the family room on the shelf."

In a few minutes a great party was happening in Hope's den — good food, good music, and good friends.

But with all the laughter, Peter felt sad inside. Being in Hope's house only made him realize how much he wanted a relationship. He missed the closeness he had shared with Hope. It was over between them, but the memories were there and always would be.

He watched Olivia slow dance with Duffy. She rested her head on his broad shoulder. They looked like the perfect match. Peter tried to keep his attention on the dialogue between Mary Ellen, Hope, and Jessica.

"I wish there were some way we could teach Diana a lesson," Hope said.

"I just wish we could ship her back to California," Jessica suggested.

"You're quiet tonight, Peter," Mary Ellen said before taking a bite of her hero.

Peter shrugged his shoulders. "I was just thinking about how couples seem to match. You and Pres were both cheerleaders, and Tara and Patrick found each other, and it looks like Kate and Sean have something special."

Hope started to laugh. "I can't imagine why. They seem totally mismatched, but their relationship appears to be working."

"Wouldn't it be great," Peter said seriously, "if you could have a guaranteed date?"

"What do you mean?"

"A date that would automatically fall in love with you."

"Peter, that would take all the fun out of dating," Mary Ellen said. "I don't think I'd like to meet a guy for the first time and know that I was definitely going to fall in love with him!"

"Well, Mary Ellen, it sounds good to me," Peter said, then he drank his soda and watched wistfully as Olivia and Duffy danced.

Suddenly the phone rang. Hope said, "I'll get it. I wonder who'd call this late."

CHAPTER

3

At the Pizza Palace, Sean, Kate, Tara, and Patrick chose a table that looked out to Main Street. The girls slid in first and unzipped their jackets.

"A large pizza with the works," Patrick called to the waitress as she passed.

Sean took off his bright red scarf and tied it around Kate's neck, letting the ends hang in the back. "Das is the Red Baron of St. Cloud," he said with a phony German accent.

"Cut it out, Sean," Kate said as she untied the scarf.

"Can't take your school losing, old girl?" Sean teased.

"I really don't care, Sean," Kate said. "I went to the game to see you cheer."

"Don't you have any school spirit?" Tara asked. She was one hundred percent committed to Tarenton High, and the idea of someone not really caring if her school won or lost shocked her.

"I care about the debating team winning, and I care about St. Cloud's academic rating in the state," Kate said, adjusting her glasses. She glanced at Sean's hurt expression, "and I care about you!"

Sean grinned.

"But don't let it go to your head. It's big enough already, Sean Dubrow," Kate added quickly.

"Sometimes I wonder why you two date each other. You seem so mismatched," Patrick said.

"Chemistry," Sean said.

Kate often wondered why she was attracted to Sean. She had a lot more in common with Ted Miller. He was witty and intelligent, and they had classes together at St. Cloud. But something was missing. Sean was exciting and a lot more fun to be with, even if he didn't have a serious bone in his body. Somehow, the combination worked. They had been dating for months.

"What do you kids want to drink with your pizza?" the waitress asked, abruptly ending the conversation at the table.

They ordered Cokes.

"I think I'll call Hope's house," Tara said. "Maybe she's home by now. I feel a little guilty about not going there with the others." Patrick moved aside to let her out of the booth.

"I feel funny about not going, too," Sean admitted.

Patrick looked at the worried expressions on his friends' faces. "I'm sure there's a simple explanation," he said reassuringly.

Tara walked over to the pay phone on the wall near the cashier. I hope they're home, she said to herself as she put the quarter into the slot and dialed. She listened as the phone rang.

"Hello," a voice said.

"Is that you, Hope?" Tara asked ecstatically.

"Tara!"

"Hope! Are you all right?"

"Yes. My brother hurt his arm, so I had to take him to the hospital. I called, but Diana didn't give Mary Ellen the message," Hope explained.

"I'd like to toast that girl on a stick," Tara said angrily.

"Listen, the kids are here. How about coming over?"

"Great idea. See you later."

The smile on Tara's face forecast the good news to her friends.

"She's okay," Tara said immediately. "Everyone's at Hope's house, and we're invited over."

"Let's get the pizza to go," Sean suggested as he signaled the waitress.

In fifteen minutes, the cheerleaders were together in Hope's family room. Duffy put on soft music, and the spread on the table looked like a feast for an army. Everyone was relieved to see Hope.

Mary Ellen looked at the group. I wish Pres

were here, she thought, instead of at his parents' home on Fable Point. It's like old times, when we're with the cheerleaders.

Monday was a clear spring day. Peter slipped a cherry-red sweater over his white shirt. He stepped back and looked at his reflection in the mirror. "Why can't you find the right girl, Peter Rayman?"

"Peter, I'm going to work," his mother called from the door. "We're out of milk for breakfast, so make yourself some frozen french toast."

" 'Bye, Mom," Peter called.

As Peter drove up to Tarenton High School, he felt a surge of pride. It was a beautiful school, built into a hill. The front of the building had three stories, and the back, five. The rear windows overlooked Narrow Brook Lake, a sight that often lulled Peter into daydreaming during English class.

Next year was an unknown quantity. He had blown a lot of the money his mother had given him from a small inheritance, and he'd probably go on to Tarenton Community College.

Peter took Computer Science with Mr. Ryan first period. He slipped behind his desk and tried to concentrate on the assignment being written on the blackboard.

Ken Harper, a lanky, baby-faced junior, leaned forward to speak to him. "Great win, this weekend, Peter."

"Hi, Ken. Were you at the game?"

"Sure, wasn't everyone? The cheerleaders

were terrific. I wish I were athletic," Ken admitted sadly.

"Cheer up, Ken, you're a computer whiz."

"What good does it do me with the girls?"

Peter tried not to smile.

"I bet the girls are all over you," Ken said enviously. "The girls on the squad are gorgeous."

"And spoken for," Peter said as he opened his loose-leaf notebook to the divider that read "Computer Science."

"All of them?"

"Sort of, except Jessica and Melissa. Jessica claims she's off men and Melissa and I are just good friends."

Ken listened intently to everything Peter said.

"Being a jock isn't everything," Peter admitted.

"I can't get a date," Ken replied. "All the girls I talk to want to be 'friends' only. It's a drag."

"I know how you feel," Peter said.

"You do?" Ken sounded amazed.

"I have plenty of girlfriends, but what I want is a *girlfriend*. It seems to me that the whole world is going two by two. Tarenton High is like Noah's Ark," Peter said sarcastically.

"Yeah, isn't it?" Ken said.

Peter looked at Ken. He had nice features, but he didn't look sixteen. His round face was smooth and a few freckles merged together over the bridge of his nose. He still wore braces, but his smile was full and friendly. It was his body that needed work. He was thin and under-developed.

Mr. Ryan faced the class. "The term is half over and everyone is familiar with our computers and the available software. I decided that it would be fun to have you use your imaginations by developing your own programs."

Some groans went up from the back of the room.

"We'll start by choosing partners, then spend the remainder of this period discussing what type of program you'd like to develop."

"Can we make up a computer game?" Randy asked.

"Yes. But it must be an original game. I don't want to see twenty versions of Pac Man," Mr. Ryan said firmly.

"Gotcha, Mr. Ryan," said Randy.

Peter leaned over and whispered to Ken. "How about being my partner?"

"Sure thing." Ken was flattered by the offer.

"All right, class. If you have any questions, I'll be at my desk," Mr. Ryan said as he opened a computer manual and put on his glasses.

Ken pulled his desk closer to Peter's. "Got any ideas?"

"Not really. You're the computer genius," Peter said, and he mentally visualized an easy A on his report card.

"Well," he said shyly, "we could create an intergalatic war game."

"I'd like to do something more practical . . . like create the perfect girl."

"We could draw one by using the picture

parts, but I don't think computer graphics are what Mr. Ryan wants," Ken said seriously.

"Besides, I don't want a computer drawing of a perfect girl. I want the perfect girl for me at Tarenton High."

Suddenly Ken's face exploded with a smile. "You want the computer to find the perfect girl for *you?*"

"You've got it, Ken!"

"We could do it!"

"How?"

"Computer dating!" Ken said enthusiastically. "We could devise a program that would match you with the perfect girl."

"Give me five!" Peter exclaimed.

Mr. Ryan looked up from his book and smiled. "I like to see enthusiasm, but keep it down, boys."

"How do we do it?" Peter asked.

"Well, to make it simple, we have to feed data into the computer and decide how the matching will work." Ken started writing in his notebook. "We'll need to get data on the girls in the matching pool."

"How many?"

"As many as you want, but we'll have to have qualifications," Ken said.

"First, all the girls have to attend Tarenton High. I don't want to have to drive back and forth between schools like Sean does to see Kate. And I don't want to date freshmen."

Ken wrote down Peter's comments.

Mr. Ryan interrupted the class. "I'd like each team to tell me what their program plans are before the end of class, so that I can approve them. Is anyone ready?"

Peter looked at Ken and smiled. They both raised their hands. Mr. Ryan walked over to their desks.

"What's your idea, boys?" he asked.

"We're going to find the perfect date for Peter." Ken described their basic idea using computer jargon, and Peter smiled.

Mr. Ryan nodded his head approvingly. "Computer dating sounds like a good idea, but I think you should expand it to include other young men, not just Peter. It isn't fair to have all these girls participate with only the possibility of one person to date."

"I see your point," Ken said seriously.

Peter felt a little disappointed. "What do you suggest, Mr. Ryan?"

"Get a good cross sample of boys and girls. Create a questionnaire and feed the data into the computer after you develop the program. I think you have a good idea."

"Thanks," Peter said as Mr. Ryan walked away. "Do you think you can do it, Ken?"

"Sure, but I want to be in the matching pool."

"Of course," Peter said, slapping his back.

Ken looked straight at Peter. "I want to date a cheerleader."

"Sure, if the computer fixes you up with a cheerleader!" Peter said.

"You don't get it, Peter," Ken said. "The computer will probably fix me up with someone like me. I want to go out with a cheerleader."

"Ask one out," Peter suggested.

"I can't. I'm too shy, and besides, she'd laugh at me. But if the computer says we're compatible, I've got a chance."

"How are you going to arrange it then?"

"Fix the computer," Ken whispered.

"You're kidding."

"Nope. Let me go with you to a practice and I'll pick the cheerleader I want to date. Then we'll give her the questionnaire, and I'll rig it so that we're matched."

"That's crooked!"

"Peter, if you want me to set up the program, get me a cheerleader to date."

"Sure . . . sure . . . anything, so that *I* find the perfect girl," Peter assured him.

"Okay. Let's get to work on the questionnaire!"

CHAPTER

Peter was surprised to discover that he enjoyed working with Ken. He didn't know Ken well enough to make a fair judgment, but somehow he had subconsciously thought that someone with a lot of brains and very little brawn had to be dull. The opposite was true. Ken was shy at first, but once Peter started working with him at his home, his unique sense of humor emerged.

The Harper home was in Baker Hill, a section outside of town which had few houses and a lot of acreage. Mr. Harper owned a dry cleaning store on Main Street, but his hobby was restoring classic Volkswagens. His backyard was filled with Beetles in various stages of repair. Mrs. Harper was a homemaker in charge of the three Harper children, the apple orchard, and her growing homemade applesauce business.

Peter followed Ken upstairs. Before Ken entered his bedroom, he pulled an outside lever. The door opened automatically, the lights went on, and the compact disc started playing a Grateful Dead song.

"Amazing!" Peter said.

"I have other things wired, too," Ken said proudly. Once inside the room, Ken went to the switchboard on his cluttered desk. Wires of different colors were attached to switches and buttons. "I can answer the door downstairs, talk to my mother in the kitchen, and even tell who's in the driveway without going to the window."

"You're kidding!"

"Nope," Ken said with a wide grin. He bounced on his bed, taking the switchboard with him. "I bugged the cars and my brother's and sister's bikes."

Peter sat down on the edge of the bed, and Ken continued to tell him about his electronic achievements. "I can turn the computer on and off from anywhere in the room."

"Can you break into programs? Remember that movie with Matthew Broderick?" Peter asked with a mischievous tone.

"Yes, but I'm not going to change grades or order stuff. I want to go to MIT, not federal prison!"

"Just kidding, Ken. Finding the perfect date for me *and* getting an A in class will be enough!" Peter walked over to the computer. "How do we start?"

"Well, this is my theory. In fact, you gave me

the idea when you said the school's like Noah's ark," Ken said seriously. He followed Peter to the computer.

"I don't get it!" Peter stared blankly at Ken.

"Two by two."

"Sure . . . one girl . . . one guy," Peter stated and shrugged his shoulders. He wanted to say "big deal," but he didn't want to hurt Ken's feelings.

"But they were paired by similarities . . . two of a kind . . ."

Peter knew it was clear to Ken, but it wasn't to himself. "Sure, two lions . . . two zebras."

"You see, we have to match boys and girls by similar interests and priorities," Ken said excitedly. "We have to make up a questionnaire based on order of preference, and then the computer will pair the couples by similarities."

"I got it!" Peter's face exploded in a smile. "If a girl says she's into sports, music, and boys, she's for me."

Ken laughed. "We'll need more information than that to make a good match. We'll have to create a section for physical characteristics, too. We don't want the girls' volleyball captain paired with the shortest guy on the tennis team."

"Agreed." Peter reached for a pad and pencil. "What's the priority stuff you mentioned?"

"Well, I thought it would be a good idea to create a list and have each person put the words into their own order of preference," Ken said seriously.

"What words?"

"Well, remember there isn't any right or

wrong," Peter agreed. "The words would be family, country, religion, money, appearance, health, education. Things like that. This way, we'll know a little more about the person than just his or her activity preference," Ken said.

"Good idea," Peter said. "Let's get going!"

On Sunday, Ken and Peter finished the questionnaire. The survey population was to be composed of sixty names, split between boys and girls in the junior and senior classes.

"I'll start out by giving them to the cheerleaders after practice on Monday," Peter said proudly as he looked at the neat pile of copies on Ken's desk.

"Good idea, and I'll give them out to the debating team."

"Okay . . . and I'll take the dramatic club. There are some really interesting girls in Thespians," Peter offered eagerly.

"Peter, we have to keep it even, boys and girls. So remember, mark off male or female on the list when you give them out."

"No sweat," Peter said enthusiastically.

Before cheerleading practice, Peter knocked on Mary Ellen's office door.

"Come in," Mary Ellen said. "Hello, Peter. What's up?"

"I have a project for Computer Science class and I'd like to talk to the cheerleaders together before practice. I have a questionnaire to give out," Peter said happily.

"Sure, you can talk to them, but I don't want

to take time away from practice to fill out the questionnaires," Mary Ellen replied. She leaned over the desk to try to read the heading on the papers. "Is there one for me to fill out, too?"

Peter laughed. "No, you're married."

"What kind of a questionnaire is this?"

"You'll see," Peter said and left quickly.

The cheerleaders came into the gym and started their individual warm-ups. Olivia, dressed in gray sweatpants and a kelly-green leotard, was describing arm positions to Melissa as they walked into the empty room. Sean and Peter, both in trim gray warm-up suits with Tarenton written on the back, entered from the boys' locker room. Tara, Jessica, and Hope followed, each dressed in colorful leotards, tights, and red-and-white school jackets. When Mary Ellen joined the group, everyone stopped talking and looked up, waiting for the coach to make the usual comments and announcements.

"Our next game is with Deep River, and they have a strong cheerleading squad. I've decided not to do response cheers. Instead, we'll go with group cheers and some really spectacular tumbling."

The cheerleaders nodded their approval.

Mary Ellen continued describing the cheers for the next basketball game. Then she announced that Peter had something to tell everyone. The gym grew quiet.

Peter felt anxious as he stood up and faced the squad. "I'm doing a research project for Mr.

Ryan's computer science course with Ken Harper, and I'd like everyone to be part of it."

"What's the project about?" Hope asked. She was surprised that Peter was interested in research.

"Any *girls* involved?" Sean shouted out good-naturedly.

Peter looked away nervously. He wasn't comfortable describing the project because he was afraid they'd laugh. Peter cleared his throat and looked into his friends' faces.

"Actually, Sean, it does concern girls. Ken Harper and I have developed a program that will pair everyone entered into a computer with his or her perfect match." No one laughed. "We're selecting thirty guys and thirty girls from Tarenton High to fill out the questionnaires. The material will be fed into the computer. After the match is completed, a printout will be processed and given to everyone."

"It's computer dating," Hope said.

Peter felt defensive. "Not really. It's just matching boys and girls by interest. You don't have to make a date with your match unless you want to."

"Forget it," Tara said quickly. "I'm in love with Patrick. We're a perfect match."

"But aren't you curious, Tara? There might be someone else at school that is just right for you," Peter said.

Tara twisted her engagement ring on her finger. "I know everyone, anyway."

"That's the point," Peter said quickly. "You

think you know everyone, but sometimes you only know the name or the face, and not his or her interests or priorities."

"Peter's right," Hope said. "A well-written questionnaire can tell you a lot about a person. Can I see one?"

"Sure." Peter was relieved to get support. "I have copies in my locker. I'll give them to you after practice."

"I'll take one blonde interested in romance," Sean said jokingly. "But don't tell Kate!"

"Well," Olivia said, "I have enough problems dating Duffy *and* Walt. I don't need a third guy in my life."

"But Walt and Duffy don't go to THS. Wouldn't you be interested in knowing if there was someone right here who is your perfect match?" Peter felt desperate. "Listen, everyone, you have nothing to lose and you could have a lot of fun!"

Mary Ellen interrupted. "After practice, Peter will be giving out the questionnaires to anyone interested in participating, but now it's time for practice."

During the session, Melissa whispered to Peter, "I'll take a questionnaire."

"Me, too," Jessica said. "I have nothing to lose as long as I don't *have* to date the guy."

"You may want to," Peter said, hoping to generate more interest in the project.

During the final practice minutes, Peter saw Ken enter the gymnasium and take a seat in the last row of the bleachers. Peter had forgotten he had invited Ken to watch the girls on the squad.

Ken watched the squad create a low pyramid. The moment he saw the lithe, graceful girl with the straight hair pulled back into a ponytail, he couldn't get his eyes off her. She was wearing a black leotard and red gym shorts over black tights. She had a classic dancer's body. Because she was the lightest girl, she climbed to the third level of the pyramid alone and posed in an arms-out victory position. Then, at the count of three, she jumped forward, landed gracefully, and immediately slid into a split.

Ken knew he had found the girl he wanted to date. He only hoped that she wasn't in love with someone else.

After practice, Ken walked over to Peter and Olivia.

"Come on, Olivia, you're the captain of the cheerleaders. It'll look funny if you don't support a science project of one of your teammates," Peter said, putting his hands on Olivia's shoulders affectionately.

"Peter Rayman, that's an underhanded argument."

"Oh, come on, Olivia, look at it as a team activity, then," Peter said. "Here comes my partner. Ken Harper, Olivia Evans."

Ken smiled at her. "We took algebra together," he said to Olivia.

Olivia looked blankly at him.

"Olivia is my only hold-out," Peter told Ken. "Even Tara, who's engaged, said she'd go along with the project if everyone else did."

"Everyone?" Ken asked.

"Yeah. Come on, Olivia, be a sport!"

"Oh, okay, Peter, but I'm doing it for you, not for a date."

"Agreed! I'll get the questionnaires."

Ken followed Peter into the boys' locker room. "I've picked the cheerleader whom I want to date."

"Which one?"

Ken smiled. "The one on the top of the pyramid during your last cheer. She was wearing red shorts and black tights. What's her name?"

Peter hesitated for a moment before he spoke. "Melissa Brezneski."

"Melissa . . . Is she going with anyone?"

Peter shook his head. "Not that I know of. She's a junior. She joined the cheerleaders as an alternate only a few months ago."

"Melissa . . . Melissa . . . Make sure she gets a questionnaire, Peter."

Peter slapped Ken's back affectionately. "You've got it!"

CHAPTER

News about the computer project spread like ice cream on a hot day. The editor of the school paper wanted an exclusive interview with Peter and Ken. Duffy wanted the boys to appear on his radio show and discuss the outcome of the project, and there was even a phone call from the *Tarenton Lighter* asking permission to send a reporter and photographer to the school on the day the results were reported to the students. Mrs. Oetjen nixed the request. "The press can meet with the students outside of the school, but I do not want them disrupting Tarenton High," she said.

Peter was cornered by Nicole Daniels, a petite brunette, outside of his homeroom.

"Why can't I have a questionnaire?" she pleaded. She shared two classes with Peter, and he considered her a pest.

"I'm sorry, Nicki, everyone can't be in it. We

have a small cross section. . . . Maybe next time."

Peter hated saying no, especially to girls, but he had to do it. Ken constantly reminded him that they had to have an equal amount of boys and girls.

As Tara passed Peter, she pulled out her questionnaire and tossed it briskly on top of Peter's books. "I don't know why I bothered with this thing!"

"Thanks, Tara." Peter looked at the beautiful red-haired cheerleader and felt sorry for the guy that was matched with her. He doesn't have a chance, Peter thought. Tara was completely in love with Patrick. But, Peter thought, it shouldn't bother him. It was a school project, *not* a dating service, and the real goal was to find him the perfect girl.

During homeroom, some guys asked Peter how the project was going, and Nicki sulked in a corner with her friends. Peter overheard Alisia High say, "You have to be asked to participate, Nicki."

"I heard that they're only asking the kids in varsity clubs," Beth Woods said angrily. "They're elitists!"

"You're just jealous, Beth," Alisia stated coolly as she flipped open a textbook. "They gave Ron Stratton a questionnaire and he doesn't have a varsity letter."

"But he's gorgeous, and he's on the debating team!" Nicki snapped.

All the attention made Peter feel like a celebrity, and he enjoyed every moment.

                              * * *

Ken joined Peter in the noisy cafeteria for an early lunch.

"I've got sixteen questionnaires back already," Ken said happily as he dug out his brown-bag lunch from his worn knapsack.

"I have about ten," Peter said. He found his meal ticket in his wallet. "I've got to buy lunch."

"I'll come with you and get a couple of chocolate milks," Ken said as he carefully placed his brown bag next to his knapsack. "I need some extra calories."

When they reached the cashier, Diana walked across the cafeteria to get a straw. She was wearing a leather miniskirt and a soft yellow oversized sweater. She smiled at Peter as she passed.

"Who's that?" Ken asked excitedly. "Madonna's little sister?"

"No, she's more like Sean Penn's!" Peter answered sarcastically.

"Very funny, Peter," Ken said, "but you have to admit she's great-looking. Did you give her a questionnaire?"

"Absolutely not!" Peter stated emphatically.

"Hey, don't bite off my head! What did she do to you?" Ken asked. He was surprised by his friend's reaction. Peter was usually mellow and seemed to like everyone.

"She's been trying to become a cheerleader since she moved here from California," Peter started to explain as they walked back to their table. Jessica and Olivia were already there, eating yogurts.

"There's no law against that," Ken said as he

45

sat down across from Peter, next to Olivia.

"It's the way she tried to get on the squad. She's underhanded and conniving and — "

"You must be talking about Diana," Olivia interrupted.

"And insensitive," Jessica added. "She purposely didn't tell Mary Ellen that Hope had called from the hospital Friday night. We were all frantic when Hope missed the game."

"And she tried everything imaginable to get Melissa's slot as alternate cheerleader," Olivia added.

"And wanted me to fail French so that there'd be an opening," Jessica said. "She started some real ugly rumors, too."

"Sounds like a bad character," Ken said between bites of his sandwich. He thought of Diana trying to hurt sweet, beautiful Melissa, and suddenly he wanted to "fix" Diana, too. "I've got an idea!"

"What?" Peter asked.

"We'll ask her to fill out a questionnaire," Ken said seriously.

"It's not fair to match her with someone in *this* school," Jessica said, "or this planet."

"That's just it. We'll fix her up with Mr. Perfect, only he won't exist." Ken became more animated as the plan came into focus. His long thin arms waved as he sought the group's attention. "We have to give her a questionnaire."

"But we've given out all the questionnaires for girls," Peter said.

"It doesn't make a difference because she'll have a fictitious computer mate," Ken said.

46

Olivia leaned forward and spoke to Ken as though she just saw him for the first time. "I like the idea so far. What happens when you give her a computer printout with a name on it? She'll try to find him at school."

"I'll use a common first name like . . . like Bill or Mike and no last name. The printout will say that he wants to be anonymous until they meet. Then I'll set up a blind date," Ken said enthusiastically.

"And Diana will blab about him to everyone, because that's Diana," Jessica added.

"And there won't be a date!" Peter said. "Brilliant, Ken. Give me a questionnaire. I'll give it to her now." Peter stood up and looked around the crowded lunchroom to find Diana.

"Go to it," Ken said. "But get the questionnaire back by tomorrow. I want to feed the material into the computer on Wednesday. The printouts should be ready to give out on Friday."

"Gotcha," Peter said. "The sooner the better."

Duffy was waiting for Olivia after practice. "Want a lift home?"

Olivia pulled on her red-and-white varsity jacket and threw her knapsack over her shoulder. "Sure."

They greeted a few people as they walked down the hilly path to the parking lot. Finally Duffy asked, "How are things going?"

"Fine," Olivia answered pleasantly. She had a feeling that Duffy had something on his mind, but she was determined to play it cool.

"Uh . . . uh . . . there's been a lot of talk about the computer dating project," Duffy said hesitantly.

"I wish you wouldn't call it that. It's a computer science project, not a computer dating service," Olivia said as she got into Duffy's car and buckled the seat belt.

"I know. In fact, I asked Peter and Ken if they'd appear on my radio show this weekend," Duffy said.

"You're going to exploit them!" Olivia said.

"What's wrong with you, Olivia? I'm not exploiting them. I'm reporting the news. Remember, I'm a journalist," he said defensively.

Olivia looked out the window, avoiding Duffy's eyes.

"You're not in the project, are you?" he asked.

Olivia didn't want to answer. She felt anger welling up inside. "Why shouldn't I be?" she snapped.

"You're too sensible, and this thing is silly. You wouldn't want to be a part of it," Duffy said confidently.

Olivia's anger burst out. "Why don't you say what you really mean, Duffy?"

He was silent.

"You don't want me to be part of the computer matching project because you're jealous. It's tough enough knowing that Walt's back in town, but the idea of a new guy in my life really throws you."

"You can do anything you want, Olivia. It's

just that I thought we had a special relationship, and it seems like a waste of time," Duffy said. He revved up the engine as he waited impatiently for the light to change.

They drove in silence down Main Street. Olivia remembered Friday night at Hope's house when they slow danced and kissed good-night. She had thought that she loved Duffy, but now her feelings had changed again. It was so confusing. Whenever Duffy got possessive, she went crazy. It was the same feeling she had when her mother tried to control her life.

Duffy couldn't stand the silence. "How's school?" he finally asked. "Straight A's?"

"I hope so," Olivia said. She was glad he changed the subject. Then she switched on the radio to relieve the tension.

Olivia wondered what her perfect match would be like. She thought she knew everyone at THS, but maybe she didn't!

CHAPTER

After cheerleading practice, Peter drove over to the Harpers' house in Baker Hill. With the music blasting out of all four speakers, Peter sang along. He couldn't wait to get the results of the computer matching, and discover his "perfect" date.

The Harpers had finished dinner, but Mrs. Harper had saved a plate of food for him. Peter was immediately welcomed by everyone.

"Ken tells us that tonight is the *big* night," Mr. Harper said as he helped clear the dinner table. "If you find an extra girl, I'm available." He laughed.

"No, you're not," Mrs. Harper shouted from the kitchen good-naturedly. "You're needed here!"

"Can I watch?" Ken's younger sister, Susan, asked.

"No. Do your homework," Mr. Harper said,

saving Peter and Ken from a ticklish situation.

"Let's go up to my room," Ken said.

Mrs. Harper appeared from the kitchen and handed Peter a plate filled with fried chicken and fresh vegetables. "Ken, take a glass of milk for Peter."

"Sure, Mom."

"Your mom's great," Peter said as he followed Ken upstairs.

"Don't tell her or you'll make her head swell," Ken joked. He pushed a button and suddenly his whole room came to life as lights, music, and the computer were activated.

"What do we do first?" Peter asked as he put the plate on the end table and started to munch.

"I fed all the data into the computer this afternoon while you were at practice. All we have to do now is open each individual file by name and print it out."

"Fantastic! Let's go!"

"Alphabetically?" Ken suggested. "Starting with the girls."

"No way, José! Cheerleaders first."

"Okay. I'll start with — " he teased.

"You'll start with me!" Peter reached over and typed his name into the computer. Suddenly Peter's answers from his questionnaire appeared on the screen in a simple code.

"I know all this stuff. How do I get the match?"

Ken pushed Peter aside and rubbed his hands together like a concert pianist preparing for a performance. With exaggerated gestures, he typed, "female match . . . name"

TERRI ROGERS appeared on the screen.

Peter read the name. It was a familiar name, but he wasn't exactly sure who she was. "Now what?"

"We call up her file and print it out for you . . . to love and hold and cherish!" Ken opened Terri's file and pushed the print button. Within seconds, Peter was holding Terri Rogers' file information.

"This is her," he said, waving the paper in the air and kissing it. "My love, my one and only." He read the sheet quickly. "She's in Thespians."

"The drama club's honor group. I don't remember an actress by that name in any of the plays," Ken said thoughtfully.

"And she likes painting, and her first priority is school and second, family. That's the same thing that I wrote," Peter exclaimed excitedly.

"That's why you were matched," Ken said. "It's the 'birds of a feather, flock together' theory."

They both laughed. Peter carefully folded the printout and put it into his jeans pocket. "Do you have last year's yearbook? Maybe she's in it," Peter said anxiously as he scanned the bookshelves.

"Sure," Ken said, as he pulled the red-and-white book out of his bottom desk drawer. Peter grabbed it out of his hands and quickly flipped to group photographs of clubs. He looked at Thespians, but Terri wasn't listed under the picture.

Ken could instantly see Peter's disappointment. "She probably wasn't voted into Thespians until her junior year. Try the drama club's photo," Ken suggested.

Peter turned the page and saw a photo of about forty members of the club smiling into the camera. In front of the group was their banner with the classic masks of tragedy and comedy. He looked at the names. " 'Terri Rogers, 3rd row.' One . . . two . . . three . . . four. That's her!"

Ken looked over his shoulder. "She looks cute!"

"She sure does, but it isn't a clear shot. I'll give her a call tonight and make a date!"

"Slow down, Peter. Why don't you wait until she gets your printout tomorrow?"

"You're right. Waiting a day can't hurt," Peter said.

"Let's get to work on the other printouts or we'll be up all night!" Ken suggested.

"Did you work out a special printout for Diana?" Peter asked.

"You bet. She'll think that she has the perfect blind date!" Ken said proudly.

"And if I know Diana, she'll brag about him to everyone," Peter added.

They didn't finish working until after midnight, so Peter decided to sleep over at the Harpers'. The next morning, they divided up the printouts.

Peter stopped at his house to change before school. He couldn't wait to surprise the cheerleaders with the results from the computer.

* * *

Jessica Bennett listened to a French tape as she dressed. Marie, the Armstrongs' maid, had created tapes of children's stories so that Jessica could get additional ear training. It had been only a few short months ago that Jessica had problems with comprehension, but now she could easily understand the short stories.

Jessica put on some light makeup. She picked a sky-blue sweater and decided to add a matching blue ribbon for her hair. Doesn't hurt to look extra good today, she said to herself as she thought about the computer printouts Peter was going to distribute at practice today. I just might want to look up my computer match! She smiled. No way, she thought suddenly. I'm off dating for a while!

Patrick picked Tara up in his van. Leon, his dog, barked a welcome when Tara jumped into the front seat. "Hi, fellas!" She kissed Patrick on the cheek and petted Leon.

Patrick didn't respond.

"Why the long face?" she asked as she buckled the seat belt.

"Today's the day, isn't it?"

"What?"

"The day Peter gives out the computer dates." Patrick sounded depressed as he drove quickly down the street and toward the high school.

"I wish you wouldn't call it that!" Tara was surprised that Patrick was taking Peter's project so seriously. "It's a computer *science* project.

All the cheerleaders are involved. I couldn't say no."

They drove for a few blocks in silence. It made Tara very uncomfortable. "Look, I'm not going to *date* the person on my printout, even if it turns out to be Rob Lowe!"

"Are you sure . . . ?"

"Yes, I'm sure. I love you, Patrick Henley. When are you going to believe me?"

"When you're wearing a gold ring on your left hand," Patrick said.

Hope picked up Melissa on the way to school. Melissa brought up the subject of the computer project immediately.

"I can't wait to find out who I'm matched with," she told Hope. "I hope he asks me out."

Hope smiled at her friend. "You don't have to wait for him to call. You'll have his name."

"I'd never be able to call a guy first . . . unless I knew him."

"You may know him," Hope suggested. "He has to go to THS. You just might be sitting next to him every day in homeroom," Hope said.

"Are you going to call your computer date?" Melissa teased.

Hope drove a few blocks before she answered. "Well, Tony's out of town. I just don't know," she finally said.

Sean called Kate before he left for school. "Good luck on your trig exam," he said.

"Thanks. Today's the day, isn't it?"

"What day?" he asked evasively.

"Peter's big day for revealing everyone's perfect match," Kate said coolly.

"Yes, but so what? It has nothing to do with us." Sean tried to reassure her. "I'll probably be paired with a goalie on the soccer team!"

"What's wrong with that?" Kate asked.

"Are you afraid of a little competition?" Sean suggested. He knew that the idea of competition always got to Kate.

"Me? Never! Competition is the one thing that *never* phases me," Kate said angrily.

"Good."

"Is there anything else on your mind, Sean Dubrow?"

Sean thought for a moment. "Nope. Good luck again. I'll see you." He hung up the phone and grinned. He realized that Kate *was* jealous, and he liked the idea.

Olivia held the two telephone messages her mother had taken last night while she was studying in the library. One was from Walt and the other was from Duffy. She definitely wasn't in the mood to talk to Duffy after their uncomfortable ride home. She threw out Duffy's message and folded Walt's into her poetry book. Wouldn't it be funny if the guy I end up going to the senior prom with is on Peter's printout? she thought.

Peter decided to give the printouts to the cheerleaders first. "Today's the day," he said to Sean when they passed in the hall.

"Who did I get?" Sean whispered.

Peter looked blank. "I'll never tell until later — "

"Come on, we're buddies!" Sean pleaded.

"You'll have to wait. But you'll be surprised," he hinted.

A few students approached him during the day, but Peter said that he'd give them out later.

Peter stopped at the attendance office to find out Terri Rogers' homeroom. He was hoping to catch a glimpse of her before she got his name.

Mrs. Barry looked up her course card. "Homeroom 415," she said.

"Great!" Peter started to go.

"Wait, Peter," Mrs. Barry called. "She's not in school today. Her name's on the absent list."

"Oh," Peter said, showing his disappointment openly.

"Sorry," Mrs. Barry said.

Peter felt that his classes were twice as long as usual. He couldn't concentrate on anything.

After his last class, he raced to the boys' locker room to change for cheerleading practice.

"Now," Sean said, sneaking up behind him.

Peter jumped. "You spooked me, Sean. I thought I'd give the printouts to everyone at the same time."

"It's your show," Sean sighed and started changing into his sweatsuit.

Peter was ready to distribute the printouts at the squad's practice, but Mary Ellen said, "After the session, Peter."

Cheerleading practice crawled along for

everyone. Mary Ellen could sense that their minds were elsewhere.

"Where's your concentration?" Mary Ellen demanded. "I said the extra-point cheer, not the basket cheer. . . . Melissa, watch your arm positions. . . . Hope, move faster. . . . Jessica, louder, please. . . ."

Finally, Mary Ellen called time out and asked everyone to form a circle and sit down.

"Look, I know what's on your mind. Why don't I just cut the practice short and let Peter take over!"

The cheerleaders applauded.

"I've got to get the envelope from my locker," Peter said as he left the group.

The room was silent. Usually the cheerleaders would use extra time to socialize, but today they were too involved in their thoughts to make small talk. Finally, Peter returned and gave out the printouts.

"Jessica," Peter said as he handed her the paper. "Your computer mate is Adam Logan."

Jessica frowned. "Who's he?"

"Swim-team captain," Tara said quickly. "He's gorgeous!"

"But what's he like?" Jessica asked nervously.

"Read the printout," Peter suggested. He handed the next sheet to Sean and followed it quickly with one to Tara. Suddenly, both shouted the other's name.

"I'm matched with Tara!"

"And I'm matched with Sean! That's crazy," Tara said.

"That's not fair," Sean said. "I want someone I don't know." He tried to hand the printout back to Peter.

"It doesn't work that way. Sorry, Sean, but there's no trading," Peter stated firmly. "Melissa!"

Melissa didn't look at her sheet until she was seated again. "Ken Harper," she said softly. She looked puzzled.

"He's a real nice guy, Melissa," Peter said. "He did the project with me." Peter held up the last two sheets. "Hope and Olivia." The girls reached for them hesitantly.

Hope read her name and instantly her face lit up. "Matthew Nikolias . . . I know him. He's the captain of the debating team and he's in the orchestra. He plays cello," Hope said happily.

"And I have Scott Prescott," Olivia said. "Everyone knows him!"

"The hunk on the football team," Tara said.

"I wonder why the computer matched us?" Olivia said thoughtfully.

"Who did you get?" Sean asked.

"Terri Rogers," Peter said proudly. He hoped there'd be a positive response, but the cheerleaders were too involved in reading their own printouts.

"I've got an idea," Peter said. "I think it would be fun to go out on a date with your computer match. You know, sort of compare notes."

"But I know Sean," Tara said, "and I'm engaged."

"A couple of hours away from Patrick won't hurt," Peter said.

"I'm not calling Matt Nikolias. Let him call me," Hope said firmly.

"That goes for me, too," Melissa said. "When Ken gets my name, let him call me."

"And if Matt and Ken feel that you should call first, then you'll never meet each other. Look at it as an experiment. One half is the printout, and the other half is meeting your match to see if it works. I'd like everyone to go out for a few hours this weekend and then come to my place for a big blast after the Deep River game."

"What about Kate?"

"And Patrick?" Tara added.

"You can have your regular dates meet at my apartment, if you want. Come on, kids, this could really be great! Look at it as an adventure . . . a guaranteed *good* blind date."

"Okay," Jessica finally said. "I have nothing to lose. I'd like to meet Adam."

Hope, Olivia, and Melissa agreed to meet their computer dates if they called. Finally, Sean convinced Tara that they should at least go out for coffee.

"Saturday night should be very interesting," Peter told Sean as they changed into their street clothes.

"Do you think any of the dates will work out?" Sean asked as he combed his hair.

"You never know," Peter said, thinking about Terri.

CHAPTER

By noon on Friday, all the computer print-outs were distributed by Peter and Ken, with the exception of Diana's. Peter felt they should wait until after classes so that Diana wouldn't have an opportunity to look for her blind date.

The high school was buzzing with the results.

"I can't believe Sean and Tara were paired," Nicki told Peter in homeroom. "It's positively demented!"

"Why?" Peter asked.

"I don't think it's healthy for cheerleaders to date each other," she said as she turned abruptly and went to her clique of girlfriends in the back of the room.

Peter smiled to himself. He remembered when he dated Hope. It was wonderful when they were going steady, but it was definitely uncomfortable when their romance ended.

Ricky leaned over Peter's desk. "Who did you get?"

"Terri Rogers," Peter answered.

Ricky displayed the thumbs-up sign and slid into his seat. "Going to ask her out?"

"If I can find her. She's been absent," Peter said.

"Terri hangs out after school with the Thespians. They read *Backstage* together and talk about the 'thea-tah'," Richie said, mimicking an affected style of speech.

"Thanks, but I'll call her at home." The last thing he wanted to do was break into the inner sanctum of Thespians. It was an exclusive group, and the idea of dating one of them made him a little uncomfortable. He was glad he had asked Ken to see that Terri got the printout.

Hope blushed bright red the minute she entered music class and saw Matt Nikolias on the other side of the room. Besides being in the orchestra together, they were in the Advanced Music Theory and Harmony course. It was an elective that only the top musicians in the school were allowed to take.

Matt had the look of an intellectual. He had high cheekbones and deep-set, dark blue eyes. He parted his jet-black hair neatly on the side, but a stubborn piece always managed to fall over his brow when he moved quickly. His thin lips made his smile look thoughtful rather than happy.

Hope slid into her seat and tried to concentrate on class. She was just opening her music notebook when she felt someone staring at her. She looked up and saw Matt standing next to her desk.

"Hi," he said. Then he cleared his throat. "Did you get your results from the matching project?"

Hope pulled the printout from the pocket in back of her notebook.

"I found it very interesting," Matt said casually.

"I did, too," Hope said.

"Would you like to discuss the results after school today?" he said seriously.

Hope realized that Matt was protecting himself from rejection by treating the date as a scientific project.

"Good idea," Hope said, continuing his academic approach. "I have cheerleading practice after school. How about meeting me in the gym?"

"Fine," Matt said and returned to his seat. "We can go to Dopey's."

As Hope prepared for the music lesson she thought, This could be a very interesting afternoon!

Peter gave Adam Logan his printout in math class. He read it over quickly.

"Which cheerleader is Jessica? The captain?" Adam asked Peter.

"No, the captain is Olivia Evans. Jessica has the long brunette hair and does a lot of the tough tumbling stunts," Peter said. "You must know her. She's great!"

"Listen, we don't have cheerleaders at the swim meets, and I've missed a lot of the basketball games because I'm involved in my own sport!" Adam said defensively.

"Sorry," Peter said quickly, "I didn't mean to put you on the spot."

"When can I meet her?"

"Well, we have practice this afternoon. If you're not swimming, why don't you drop by?" Peter suggested.

"I just may do that!"

Peter gave Scott Prescott his computer printout outside of the football coach's office. Scott knew exactly who Olivia Evans was the moment he read her name.

"Great!" he said enthusiastically to Peter. "I've thought about calling her for a date, but Olivia always seems to have a boyfriend. . . ."

"Or two," Peter added.

"I'll try for three. This computer dating thing is really terrific," Scott said, slapping Peter on the back. "I'll call her tonight."

Peter smiled as he walked away from the football player. He liked Scott's quick, positive reaction. Scott was a likable guy and a good athlete, and Peter secretly hoped the match would work.

Just as Peter turned the corner to go upstairs, he spotted Terri Rogers. His first impulse was to turn away and avoid her. She was engrossed in conversation with a guy dressed completely in black, from his turtleneck to his shoes. Peter didn't know if she had gotten the computer results yet, so he decided to play it cool and just walk by without stopping.

She's beautiful, Peter thought as he passed her and continued toward the stairs. Her light hair had blonde highlights, and her long bangs brought out her large blue eyes. She was wearing a pastel, flowered, country-girl dress with a lace collar and a long, full skirt.

Peter's heart started to race. I'll call her tonight, he said to himself, although the idea of dating Terri made him anxious. But we're matched, he said to himself firmly. She's going to *want* to meet me.

Ken told Peter during lunch that he was going to stop in at cheerleading practice and talk to Melissa.

"It's going to be a busy practice," Peter said.

"Why?" Ken asked.

"It looks like Adam Logan is going to watch Jessica, Scott Prescott is going to watch Olivia, and Hope said Matt Nikolias is meeting her after practice. It's going to be more like a school dance than a practice!" Peter said. "Mary Ellen might be upset with all the outsiders."

"I think I'll call Melissa," Ken said. "I don't want to be part of a public scene."

"Oh, come on, Ken. It'll be all right!"

"No. Tell Melissa I'll call her at home," he said firmly. "I'd be too uncomfortable in the gym with everyone watching and listening to us. I'll feel better on the phone."

"It's up to you, Ken. Whatever makes you feel comfortable. I'll tell Melissa that you'll be calling."

"Thanks, Peter."

Mary Ellen put some lively music on the tape for warm-up exercises. The cheerleaders came out of the locker rooms one at a time or in two's and started their individual stretches and bends. First, they worked on arm reaches, head rolls, and shoulder lifts. Then they moved to body stretches and finally leg exercises. After individual warm-ups, Mary Ellen led the group in some practice jumps and leaps, and a short aerobic routine to the theme from *Flashdance*. In ten minutes, everyone was warmed up and ready to start working on group cheers.

Jessica was practicing walkovers when Tara whispered, "He's here, Jessica!"

"Who?" Jessica asked, recovering from a perfect one-armed front walkover.

"Adam Logan. He's standing near the exit," Tara said as she nodded her head over her shoulder.

Jessica didn't want to stare. "Pretend we're talking," she said to Tara as she started doing side bends with her hands on her hips. "I want to see him."

"He's built like Patrick — strong arms and broad shoulders," Tara said, describing Adam. "Nice-looking."

"Agreed, but what do you think his personality is like?" Jessica said, catching glimpses between her moves.

Tara shrugged her shoulders. "You'll have to go on a date with him to find out."

Mary Ellen took the megaphone and started to announce the next routine. "Today, I thought we'd work on partner stunts. As we've discussed, you must have total trust in your partner in order to do these stunts. Melissa, Tara, and Hope, I'd like you to be the spotters. Let's start with 'The Bird.' Jessica, I'd like you to do the cheer with Sean as your partner."

Jessica was pleased that she was chosen. It was a dramatic stunt and sure to impress Adam.

Mary Ellen explained the lift, and she had Sean and Jessica walk through the cheer before they tried it. Peter and Tara placed the mats on the floor, and Hope and Melissa took their assigned places as spotters.

"We're going to use this at the end of the next victory cheer. Let's hear the words again."

The cheerleaders started to chant:

"We've scored.
We've won.
We're number one.
Tarenton Wolves . . . let's fly!"

"On the words 'let's fly!' you're to start your run, Jessica, and fly right into Sean's arms. He'll hold you while you have your arms out as though you're flying. Are you ready?"

Jessica nodded.

"We'll practice 'The Bird.' Then we'll integrate it into the cheer."

Sean lifted Jessica a few times so that they

67

could get the feeling of the final position before they attempted the full stunt.

"I'm ready," Jessica said to Mary Ellen.

Sean nodded. The cheerleaders chanted the cheer without doing the routine. At the words, "let's fly," Jessica ran toward Sean, and just at the right moment, she glided forward. Sean caught her and lifted her into the air. For a split second, Jessica looked like she *was* flying.

The other cheerleaders applauded.

"Perfect," Mary Ellen said.

Jessica felt a wonderful surge of pride as Sean put her down.

"Now, we'll work on the group part of the cheer." Mary Ellen instructed the squad to do a set of arm movements, leaps, and cartwheels leading up to Jessica's finale.

They worked on the cheer until it was smooth. Jessica felt exhilarated each time she completed the new cheer. She had forgotten that Adam was watching her until the practice session was over and Adam walked over to her as she was leaving the gym.

"Hi," Adam said. He was smiling broadly.

He took her by surprise. "Hi!" Jessica said as she put a towel around her neck and wiped the perspiration away.

"I'm Adam Logan," he said, admiringly. "We were matched, you know — the computer dating thing."

"Yes," Jessica said. "I got your printout."

"You were really great. That last stunt was amazing!"

"Thanks," Jessica said, enjoying the flattery.

"How about going to Dopey's for a Coke?" Adam asked. "You look like you could use some cold refreshment."

Jessica laughed. "You're right. I'll be showered and changed in a few minutes."

"Great. I'll be waiting in the hall."

Jessica took extra care dressing and applying her makeup.

"I saw you talking to Adam," Tara said as she brushed her long red hair vigorously. "What did he say?"

Jessica smiled as she pulled her hair back on one side and placed a comb into it. "We're going to Dopey's."

"This guy doesn't waste time," Tara said. "Are you going to ask him to Peter's party tomorrow night?"

"Maybe," Jessica said as she applied a little more blush to her cheeks. "Got to go. Adam's waiting outside." Jessica grabbed her book bag and started out the door.

Adam was leaning against the wall, reading the sports section of the *Tarenton Lighter*. He looked up the moment he heard footsteps.

"Ready?" he asked as he folded the paper and stuck it into his red-and-white athletic bag. "My Jeep's in the parking lot."

They walked down the hilly path to the student parking area. "How did this whole project start?" Adam asked.

Jessica told him about Peter's desire to find the perfect date and his project partner, Ken Harper. It was a comfortable conversation, and by the time they reached Adam's Jeep, Jessica felt that they were friends.

"Do you like country-western music?" Adam asked as he started the engine.

"I like it, but I don't know too much about it," Jessica admitted.

Adam turned on a local country-western station. Alabama was playing their latest hit, and Adam hummed the song for a few bars. Hanging over the radio was a mermaid attached to a string. Jessica reached up and flicked it so that it moved. Adam laughed. "That's Little Daryl. . . ."

"Little Daryl?"

"Remember the movie *Splash* with Daryl Hannah?" Adam said.

"Got it," Jessica said quickly.

The next song on the radio was sung by a country singer unfamiliar to Jessica. Adam took the opportunity to show off his knowledge about the music. By the time he had finished his lengthy talk on the subject, they arrived at Dopey's.

Adam picked a booth near the window where they could be seen and see everyone in the hangout. After they ordered large Cokes, Adam started praising Jessica's acrobatic skills.

"You were amazing. I couldn't keep my eyes off you," he said.

"Thanks."

"Do you always do the most difficult stunts?" he asked.

"Either I do them or Olivia does." Jessica sipped her Coke.

"Olivia's the captain," Adam stated, and a tiny frown crossed his face. "I was wondering, since you're the best acrobat, why aren't you the captain?"

Jessica was taken by surprise. "Olivia was voted captain."

"But shouldn't the best cheerleader have that job?"

Jessica felt uncomfortable. "I don't know. We're all good cheerleaders. It's just that the acrobatic stuff comes easier to me."

"That's the point. You're not like the others. You're better because you're the best athlete. You should be the captain," Adam said firmly.

"But . . ." Jessica paused. She felt confused by Adam's remarks, and at the same time she felt flattered.

"I'm the captain of the swim team because I'm the best swimmer. You're the best cheerleader and I think *you* should be captain," Adam explained logically.

Jessica didn't make another comment, but she kept hearing what Adam had said: "The best should be captain and *you're* the best!"

CHAPTER

Dinner was on the table when Jessica came home.

"You're late, Jessica," her mother, Abby, called from the kitchen table. "You know that Daniel likes to eat right after the six o'clock news."

"Sorry, Mom," Jessica shouted through the house as she hung up her jacket.

"Come to the table right now," Abby ordered. "Your meal is getting cold."

Jessica walked into the small dining area in the kitchen. Her stepfather, Daniel, barely looked up from his food when she entered.

"How come you're late?" Abby asked as she filled the empty dish with meat loaf and vegetables.

"I went to Dopey's," Jessica said.

"Wasting your money on food just before dinner. That doesn't make any sense to me," Daniel said.

Jessica ignored his remark and spoke directly to her mother. "I had a date with my computer match," she said cheerfully.

Abby's face brightened. "Tell me about him."

"His name's Adam Logan, and he's the captain of the swim team, a senior, and really nice," Jessica said between bites.

"Don't jump to any quick conclusions," Abby warned.

"I know. I'm not ready to jump back into the frying pan!" Mother and daughter both laughed when Jessica used her mother's favorite expression.

Just as Jessica started clearing the dinner dishes, the phone rang. Abby answered it. "It's for you, Jessica," she said and cupped the receiver. "It's Adam," she whispered.

"I'll take it upstairs," Jessica said and dashed from the room.

Jessica closed the door to her bedroom and picked up her phone. She laid down on her bed and took a deep breath before she spoke. "Hi, Adam," she said in a peppy voice.

"Hi, Jessica. How's my favorite cheerleader?" Adam said.

"Fine. I was just finishing dinner," Jessica answered.

"We don't eat until later," Adam said. Then there was a slight pause. "I was wondering if you'd like to go to the Garrison swim meet with me tomorrow morning. That's if you don't have cheerleading practice," Adam added quickly.

"No, only the game at night," Jessica said without hesitation.

"Great. Would you like to go?" Adam asked.

"Yes. I'd love to. I've never been to a swim meet," she said enthusiastically.

"Good. I'll pick you up at nine. It's pretty warm in the pool area, so wear something lightweight."

"And with 'Tarenton High' printed on it!" Jessica suggested.

"Good idea, but there won't be any cheering," Adam said candidly. "In fact, it's very different than going to a basketball game."

They continued to chat for a few minutes until Abby called Jessica to come down and help with the dishes.

Peter waited until after dinner to dial Terri Rogers' phone number. As he waited for someone to answer, he half hoped she wouldn't be home. *Why am I so nervous?* Peter asked himself. *It's silly! She has my printout also, and she's probably dying for me to call!*

"Hello," a clear, young female voice answered.

"Is Terri Rogers home?" Peter asked politely.

"I'm Terri."

Peter liked her friendly voice immediately. "This is Peter Rayman. I got your name from the computer project."

Terri gave a slight chuckle before she spoke. "You mean the computer *dating* project."

Peter felt a warm flush. "It's really only a

computer science project. Did you get the print-out with my name on it?"

"Yes, and I thought it was very interesting," Terri said coyly. "Clever idea."

"Thanks. I was wondering, would you like to meet and discuss the printout?" Peter asked nervously.

"That might be interesting. I'll tell you what. I'll be home tonight. If you'd like to stop over, we could chat," Terri suggested.

"Fine. How's nine?" Peter asked.

"Good. See you then, Peter," Terri said confidently and hung up.

Ken was taking his books out of his locker when he heard someone calling his name.

"Ken Harper, wait!"

Ken turned around and saw beautiful, blonde Diana Tucker running toward him. "Wait!" she said breathlessly.

Ken was taken by surprise. "Hi," he said awkwardly. He wasn't used to attractive girls shouting his name in the halls.

"I didn't get my computer printout," Diana said when she finally reached him. "Do you have it?"

"Yes, of course," he stammered as he reached into the folder stuck in his notebook. "I almost forgot," he said, handing it to her.

Diana smiled as she looked at the paper. "He's athletic . . . and very smart . . . and likes romance! Great!" Suddenly she stopped and examined both sides of the sheet. "There's no name on the printout!"

"Oh, you have a very unusual situation. Your computer match wants to remain anonymous," Ken said casually.

"But how can I meet him if I don't know who he is?" Diana said angrily. "I *must* have his name," she demanded.

"I promised, Diana. Sorry," Ken said.

"You can't do this to me. It's not fair, Ken. He has my name and my printout," Diana said furiously.

Ken nodded his head in agreement. "I know it isn't fair and I argued the point with him, too. He said that he wants a blind date with you. Something very private. He said he'd call you and arrange everything."

Diana stared at Ken as though she wanted to murder him on the spot. "He'd better call me and soon, or you're dead!" She turned abruptly and walked down the hall.

Ken took a deep breath and looked down at the only other printout in the folder. It was Melissa's and he had her telephone number written on the top.

As soon as Ken arrived home, he called Peter.

"I gave the printout of Diana's computer match to her," Ken said to his partner. "It almost blew her mind when she didn't get his name. I thought she was going to strangle me."

"I wish I had been there to see her face," Peter said with a chuckle.

"What's the rest of the plan? I said her date would call," questioned Ken.

"And he will," Peter said confidently. "I'll do

76

it tomorrow and disguise my voice."

"Then what?" Ken asked.

"Set up the blind date," Peter answered. "No sweat, Ken. I have it all figured out. Now, what about you and Melissa? Have you asked her to my party yet?"

Ken hesitated.

"Are you there, Ken? Date . . . Melissa . . . Party . . . ?" Peter said, trying to gently push his new friend.

"I don't know. I rigged the computer. Maybe we aren't right for each other," Ken said.

"You're not going to get out of this. Melissa expects you to call her. I told her at practice, and she's looking forward to it."

"Did she say so?" Ken asked anxiously.

"Ken, I know Melissa. The two of you are going to hit it off. Believe me. Call her the minute you hang up with me."

Ken envied what appeared to be Peter's confidence and easy, relaxed way with girls.

"Promise to call Melissa, *now!*" Peter urged.

"Okay," Ken finally relented.

"Call me after you speak to her," Peter said and hung up.

Ken sat on the edge of his bed as he dialed Melissa's number. The phone rang and his heart pounded in his chest.

"Hello," Melissa answered.

"Hi, Melissa? Ken . . . Ken Harper," Ken said nervously.

"Oh, hello. How are you?" Melissa replied in a pleasant voice.

"Fine. I have your printout from the com-

77

puter," Ken said, mustering up a little more confidence.

Melissa laughed. "I have yours, too. It was very interesting. I didn't know you liked dance."

"Oh, sure. I went to *The Nutcracker* in Minneapolis last Christmas with my family and I thought it was fabulous," Ken said.

"Me, too. I love the ballet," replied Melissa.

"You're so graceful, I wonder, do you want to be a ballerina?" Ken asked.

"Not anymore, but I used to dream about it. I think a lot of little girls dream about becoming ballerinas. I've been studying modern dance," she continued.

"Oh," Ken said, his voice sounding disappointed. He didn't know anything about modern dance. For a while the conversation halted until Melissa switched the subject to cheerleading, and Ken was able to talk about basketball.

"I never really appreciated cheerleading until I tried acrobatics in gym," Ken said, more relaxed now. "I couldn't keep my legs straight when I did a cartwheel!"

Melissa laughed. "My brother is a karate nut and he thought tumbling was for babies until he tried it."

"I'm looking forward to watching you tomorrow night at the Deep River game," Ken said a little shyly.

"I might not be in many of the cheers. I'm only an alternate," Melissa said.

"I know, but I'll be watching only you." Ken couldn't believe he had just told a girl that he was interested in her.

"Thanks . . . I'll do my best," Melissa said.

"I wondered . . . I mean . . . after the game . . . Peter is going to have a party for the computer matches, and I thought . . ." Ken faltered.

"Yes, I'd love to go," Melissa added to his half-finished question.

"Great! Terrific!" Ken said excitedly. "I'll see you after the game. 'Bye."

" 'Bye, Ken," Melissa said sweetly.

Ken did a somersault on his bed and almost fell over the edge. "I have a date with Melissa! I have a date with Melissa!" he shouted.

CHAPTER

Peter couldn't concentrate on his math homework. He kept watching the clock and rereading the computer printout about Terri Rogers. His mother, Fran, was in the next room watching TV.

Their relationship had survived the stormy incident in which Peter bought a sports car his mother disapproved of, but every once in a while she'd still put in a dig about it.

"I've got to go out," Peter said as he entered the small living room.

Fran looked at her watch and frowned. "At this hour? It's almost nine."

"I'll only be out for about an hour or so. I'm going over to Terri Rogers' house," he said, avoiding giving her additional information.

Something on the TV drew Fran's attention back to the screen. "Okay, but drive carefully!"

"I'll be back early," Peter said as he left the house.

Peter drove slowly to the exclusive Fable Point section of Tarenton, where Terri lived. He thought about taking her to the senior prom. She'd be the Prom Queen, and he'd be the envy of every male student in the school.

Peter checked the addresses carefully when he pulled into Clover Drive. Terri's house was the ranch in the cul-de-sac. The front light was on and Peter parked right in front of the house.

Peter checked his hair in the rearview mirror and, because he was nervous, made a funny face. The chilly night air made him walk quickly to the front door. He rang the bell and waited impatiently, shifting from foot to foot, until the door opened.

Mrs. Rogers appeared. She was a petite, blonde woman, immaculately dressed in tailored slacks and a heather-colored sweater set. Her smile was forced. "Yes?" she said coolly.

"I'm Peter Rayman. I've come to see Terri," Peter explained. There was a moment's hesitation before Mrs. Rogers indicated that he should come in.

"It's Peter, dear," Mrs. Rogers called as she disappeared down the hall and left Peter standing alone in the circular foyer.

Peter looked into the living room. It was furnished in white, silver-gray, and chrome. Peter thought it looked like it could be featured on *Lifestyles of the Rich and Famous*. While he waited, he glanced at the print hanging in the foyer.

"Like it?" Terri said from behind him.

Peter turned and nodded, but his focus had switched to the beautiful girl standing in front of him.

"It's signed by Lichtenstein," Terri pointed out. Peter was too stunned by Terri's beauty to comment. "Lichtenstein, as in Roy Lichtenstein, the pop artist?" Her light blue eyes twinkled, and when she smiled, a dimple appeared in one cheek.

Peter nodded in agreement.

"Let's go into the den," Terri said as she turned away from the colorful print. Peter followed her. "You did write on the questionnaire that you liked painting?"

When they entered the black and white family room, Peter waited for Terri to sit on the oversized black leather sectional before he sat next to her.

Terri looked at him. He realized that she was waiting for an answer related to painting. "Oh, painting . . . I meant painting things. I've made some extra money painting rooms, and it's fun," he said feeling embarrassed.

"Oh," Terri said. "I guess the questionnaire didn't qualify the answers well enough."

Peter wasn't sure about what she meant by "qualifying." "Ken Harper worked on the project with me."

"I know Ken. He's very bright," Terri added. "And I've seen you around the halls and at the games."

Peter didn't want to admit that even though she was so pretty, he hadn't noticed her. "And

I've seen you, too," he hesitated, then added, "but not in any plays. Which plays have you been in?"

Terri laughed. "None, Peter. I haven't been *in* the school plays."

Peter was confused. "But you're a Thespian . . ."

"A behind-the-scenes Thespian, not an actress. I design the sets and build them."

"But you're so . . . so pretty," Peter said. "You should be the star!"

"Thanks, but I don't want to be a star. I don't think it's as creative as taking a barren stage and turning it into a setting. From nothing to something, that's what it's all about to me."

Peter agreed.

"I wonder why we were paired," Terri said as she reached for her printout and read it. "You said you like beautiful things, physical activity, cars, painting."

Peter looked at his printout. "You also checked beauty, physical activity, and painting . . . but no cars!"

They both laughed, and again there was silence until Terri asked, "Would you like a Coke?"

"Sure, thanks."

While Terri was in the kitchen, Peter looked around the room. It was very different from the crowded apartment he shared with his mother. The Raymans' furniture was made of wicker, which was now quite worn, and the only magazines on the coffee table were *TV Guide* and *People*. The Rogers' home was impeccably decorated, and copies of *Architectural Digest, The New Republic,* and *Vogue* were lying on the glass coffee table.

Terri returned with two glasses of soda and a bowl of nuts balanced on a teak tray. "It's a regular Coke," Terri said. "My family doesn't believe in using artificial sweeteners."

"I agree," Peter stated. He thought that at least they had one thing in common, even if it hadn't appeared on the printout. "My mother works at Tarenton General Hospital and she's very concerned about nutrition."

Terri sat down gracefully on the couch. "Tell me about cheerleading," she said.

Peter was delighted to switch the conversation to a subject he knew well. Without hesitation, he told her all about the cheerleading squad, and why he enjoyed cheerleading. Then he spoke about Coach Engborg's move to California and Mary Ellen's appointment as cheerleading coach. Terri told him that she had always admired Mary Ellen when she was the captain of the squad.

"Mary Ellen and Pres were the perfect couple!" Terri said.

"They're married now," Peter continued. "Pres works for his father and Mary Ellen is going to Tarenton Community College at night."

"It sounds like they have it together!" Terri added.

"You know, Terri, you would have made a terrific cheerleader. You're vivacious and pretty and — "

"Stop it, you'll make my head swell," she interrupted. Then she looked at her watch. "It's getting late, and I have to get up early tomorrow to paint flats for the next drama club production."

"Are you planning to go to the basketball game Saturday night? It's against Deep River," Peter asked as he finished the soda and put the glass on the tray.

"I don't have any plans," Terri answered coquettishly.

"Well, there's going to be a party at my apartment after the game for all the cheerleaders and their computer-matches. Would you like to come?" Peter asked, forcing himself to sound confident.

"Sure, why not?" Terri said as she placed her glass back on the tray and stood up.

Peter rose and realized for the first time how much taller he was than Terri. It made him feel protective. He looked down at her smiling face and said, "Great. I'll meet you after the game."

During the drive home, Peter thought about Terri. She was everything he had always thought he wanted in a girl, but something wasn't right. She was beautiful, full of energy, and she was definitely a brain. The computer said that they should be the perfect match, but he doubted it. Something about her made him insecure, and he didn't like the feeling.

A message, "Call Scott Prescott — 878-4510," was held by a Snoopy magnet on the Evans' refrigerator. Olivia smiled to herself as

85

she poured a glass of skimmed milk.

Scott had the reputation for being a nice guy, and Olivia felt comfortable returning his call.

She relaxed on the den sofa and dialed the Prescotts' number.

"Hi, Scott! Olivia Evans," she said as though they were old, old friends.

"Hi, Olivia. I have it in writing that we were meant for each other," Scott said with a chuckle.

"Good opening line, Scott."

"I thought of it the moment I saw the computer printout," he admitted proudly. "I just wanted you to know that I'm not a dumb jock."

Olivia laughed. "I try never to stereotype."

"Then we're off to a good start," Scott said. "How about it if I pick you up and we go for pizza and a flick tonight?"

"You move pretty quickly," Olivia said cheerfully.

"You have to be fast when you play varsity ball! What do you say?"

"Fine . . . but let's go dutch treat. This is part of a scientific experiment, not a real date!"

"No problem. To me, a date is a date, but dutch treat sounds good this time! I'll be over in a half hour."

After a quick good-bye, Olivia realized she had to hurry if she wanted to meet Scott dressed in a fresh outfit and makeup.

Olivia scribbled a quick note to her mother explaining that she wouldn't be home for dinner. Then she dashed upstairs to change into her favorite slacks and sweater. She took extra time with her eyeliner and blusher. She was still brushing her hair when the doorbell rang.

Quickly she pulled her hair to one side and put a large blue plastic comb into it to hold it in place.

"Coming!" she shouted as she raced down the stairs. Before she answered the door, she took a deep breath to compose herself. Then she opened the door and smiled at the tall, friendly boy standing at the door, holding a small bunch of daffodils wrapped in brightly decorated paper. He handed the flowers to Olivia.

"These just came up in our garden," he said, handing her the yellow flowers.

"Oh, they're lovely. The first flowers of spring," Olivia said with pleasure. "Come in; I'll put them in water."

Scott followed Olivia into the kitchen. He watched her closely as she cut the ends, so that the flowers were even, and placed them in a vase. She then placed the vase in the center of the round kitchen table.

"Thanks," Olivia said sweetly as she admired the flowers. "It was very thoughtful." She detected a faint blush on Scott's face.

Scott had a babylike face on a grown man's body. His cheeks were full and his curly hair was unruly. He was bigger than Duffy and Walt, but he looked like their kid brother.

"I thought we'd go to the Pizza Palace and then see the new Tom Cruise movie," Scott suggested when they got into his black Trans Am. It was an old model but in perfect condition.

Scott immediately turned the tape deck on full blast, making it impossible to converse as they drove. It wasn't until they were seated at the Pizza Palace that they began to talk.

"I was surprised at our match," Scott said. Then he quickly added, "Pleasantly surprised. I *never* thought I'd get the captain of the cheerleaders!"

Olivia was flattered, but as Scott spoke she realized that he was insecure. In fact, he seemed nervous.

"Let's compare printouts," Olivia suggested when the conversation slowed down. Olivia placed the two papers side by side on the table. They carefully studied the material, and suddenly they pointed to priorities.

"We both put health first," Olivia noted with a questioning look at Scott. "I bet we're the only two kids in the group that put health as our number-one priority."

Scott looked away, and Olivia could sense his discomfort. Her voice softened as she spoke. "I had a heart problem when I was a kid."

Scott looked at her with disbelief. "You?"

"Yes, me," she admitted, "and an over-protective mom, which didn't help."

"I'd never have guessed. You look so healthy," Scott said.

Olivia laughed. "I am healthy . . . *now*, but when I was little, I wasn't. Health couldn't be more important to me," she continued seriously. Then she waited for Scott to explain his answer on the printout. It took him a while to speak, but Olivia was patient, and soon Scott started.

"I didn't mean to get so serious on the questionnaire. I guess it just came out," he said hesitantly.

Olivia nodded and reached across the table to touch his hand for encouragement.

"It still bothers me to talk about it," he said. Just at that moment the waitress placed the pizza on the table. It interrupted a special moment, and they stopped speaking. When the waitress left, Scott was more in control.

"My brother died just before we moved to Tarenton three years ago. In fact, that's why we moved. My parents wanted to get away from the place that had such bad associations. We were living in Boston because there was this great children's hospital there and they wanted Andy to have the best care," Scott said.

"What did he have?" Olivia asked gently.

"A genetic disease that affects the lungs. It got worse and worse as he got older. He died when he was my age, seventeen. I looked at the list of priorities on the questionnaire, and nothing seemed important except health," Scott said as he looked into Olivia's eyes. Suddenly, his expression changed as he took a slice of pizza. "Better eat before the pie gets cold." He forced a smile on his face.

Olivia knew their special moment was over. They discussed movies and school and never returned to anything personal. By the time they arrived at the movie theater, they were talked out, and Olivia was happy to relax and watch the film.

"Do you want to stop for something?" Scott asked as they walked out of the theater.

"No, thanks," Olivia said. "I'm stuffed from the pizza and the popcorn, and tomorrow's a long day."

Scott took her hand as they walked back to his car. Olivia hoped that she wouldn't bump into Duffy or Walt, and she didn't want rumors to start, suggesting that she was interested in Scott, too. Unfortunately, a little hand-holding could go a long way on the gossip mill.

They listened to the radio on the drive back to the Evans' house. Scott walked her to the door.

"I'd like to see you again," Scott said as Olivia unlocked the front door.

She turned and faced him. "After the game, tomorrow night, Peter is giving a party for the computer matches. Would you like to come?"

"Sure . . . great," Scott said. "I'll see you at the game!"

As Scott turned to leave, Olivia closed the front door. She leaned against it and thought, what am I doing? I have enough problems with Duffy and Walt. I don't need another guy in my life!

CHAPTER

Adam's Jeep was in front of the Bennett house at exactly two minutes to nine on Saturday morning. Jessica was watching for him through her bedroom window. She was wearing sleek light-blue jeans and an oversized red-and-white Tarenton High T-shirt, which she had tied at the bottom into a tight knot.

Jessica switched off her tape deck, grabbed her Tarenton High School varsity jacket, and raced down the stairs. She opened the door just as Adam rang the bell. When the door flew open and they stood face to face, they both laughed.

"Magic doorbell!" Adam joked.

"I saw you through the window," Jessica said.

Adam took Jessica's arm and steered her gently toward the Jeep. There was something about Adam's action that was very possessive, and Jessica pulled back slightly. "Got to hurry," he said with a big smile as she opened the door on the passenger side. "I'll put the top down, if you don't think you'll be cold."

"Great. It's a beautiful day!" Jessica said. She wished she had brought a scarf to protect her hair, but she settled for zipping up her jacket and keeping her long hair under the collar.

Adam reached over and tightened Jessica's seat belt. "Jeeps tend to bounce a little more than cars. I want you safe and sound!"

Jessica flashed him a dazzling smile as he started the Jeep. "Let's go, Tarenton High, let's go!" she cheered as they started to drive to the rival school in Garrison.

The Garrison pool was in an enclosed area. Just as Adam had warned, it was hot and humid. Jessica was glad she had worn a short-sleeved T-shirt. She looked around as she waited for Adam to change into his swim trunks in the dressing room. There were no more than twenty spectators on the wooden benches, and she didn't recognize anyone. There were definitely no cheerleaders in sight.

Jessica felt a tap on her shoulder. "Hi!"

Jessica turned around and saw Duffy. He had his camera around his neck and a big, friendly smile on his face. "What are you doing here?"

"I'm with Adam Logan," Jessica said. She could tell from his face that he was surprised. "He's my computer match," she explained.

"Maybe there's a story here," Duffy said as he started to focus his camera on Jessica.

Jessica turned away from the camera. "Cut it out, Duffy. This isn't really a date. I've never been to a swim meet before and I thought it would be interesting."

Duffy put the camera down. "Okay, but how about going on my radio show and discussing the computer dating project."

"No. Absolutely not," Jessica answered emphatically.

Duffy sat down next to her on the bench. "Who did Olivia get?" he asked seriously.

"Scott Prescott," Jessica answered, trying to sound as casual as possible.

"Scott! They have nothing in common!"

"They must have *something* in common or they wouldn't have been matched," Jessica stated. Just then Adam came toward them in red-and-white-striped racing trunks. He frowned when he saw Duffy talking to Jessica. Jessica waved to him and quickly introduced Duffy to Adam when he reached the bench, making it clear that Duffy dated Olivia.

Jessica was glad Duffy was with her during the meet because Adam was completely absorbed in the races. There were individual races and relay races. Adam's best stroke was the butterfly, but he placed in all the races he was in, whether the stroke was the crawl or the butterfly. He worked closely with the coach, and it was obvious that the other Tarenton swimmers accepted his leadership.

Duffy explained some of the swimming techniques and scoring system to Jessica, but this hardly helped to make the meet interesting to her. Although the team members cheered their teammates on, there was very little excitement compared to basketball and football games. Wins were announced and applauded and quickly forgotten as the next group of racers prepared to start.

Tarenton was victorious, and by noon, Jessica and Adam were back in the Jeep heading toward home. There was no victory celebration, which for Jessica made the win seem anticlimactic.

"How did you like the swim meet?" Adam asked as they turned out of the Garrison parking lot.

"Different," Jessica answered noncommittally.

"I told you," Adam said proudly.

Jessica nodded.

"I won the most races. I don't want to brag, but I'm the best swimmer and the guys respect me. That's why I'm the captain," Adam boasted. "Aren't you the best gymnast?"

Jessica nodded again. "I guess so."

"You should be captain, not Olivia," Adam said. "I can't wait to watch you tonight at the basketball game. Are you going to do that new cheer?"

"Yes, if we're winning," Jessica said.

"You're spectacular! You fly through the air like a bird," Adam said as he smiled at her approvingly. "Jessica, we'd make the perfect pair . . . captain of the swim team and captain of the cheerleaders. The computer was right when it matched us!"

Jessica felt confused because Adam's argument sounded logical. The best should be captain, but it didn't feel right!

They stopped for lunch at a diner outside of Tarenton. Adam continued to talk about how important it is to be a leader, not a follower, and his plans to make the swimming team at the state university the following year. "If I do well at the state level, maybe I'll try out for the Olympics," he said as they shared an order of fries and ate their sandwiches. Jessica had never dated anyone with so much ambition. Patrick was a hard worker, but his plans never extended beyond Tarenton. Adam Logan wanted the world, and he wasn't afraid to go out and fight for it!

After Adam dropped her off at home, Jessica called Tara and told her all about her date with Adam.

"I never realized how important it is to be the captain of a varsity team," Jessica told Tara after she described the swim meet. "It's a big responsibility."

"It sure isn't for me," Tara added. "All the problems seem to be dumped on Olivia's shoulders."

"But that's the point. Olivia is like the den mother. She gets all the personal problems, but Adam says the captain should be the best cheerleader."

For a moment, there was silence on the other end of the phone. Then Tara spoke. "What are you trying to say?" she asked.

"Nothing. It's just that the captain should be the best cheerleader. It shouldn't be a popularity contest. I'm not saying that Olivia isn't doing a good job, but maybe the team would do more daring stunts if she were a better gymnast," Jessica suggested hesitantly.

"Maybe," Tara said. She was a little confused by Jessica's statement.

"I'd sure like your opinion, Tara," Jessica said confidentially.

"I'll think about it," Tara said. "Listen, I have to spend an hour with Sean before the game. We promised Peter that we'd go on a 'computer date,' " Tara explained.

"Does Patrick know?" Jessica questioned without hesitation.

"Sure. We don't keep secrets from each other," Tara answered.

Jessica was surprised that Tara was willing to spend even one hour away from Patrick, especially with another guy, but then Tara was constantly surprising her. The popular redhead was the last person she thought would want to get engaged and settle in Tarenton after graduation.

"I'll see you at the game tonight. 'Bye," Jessica said as her thoughts returned to cheerleading and becoming captain of the squad.

Next, Jessica called Melissa.

"Did Ken Harper ask you out?" Jessica asked after she told Melissa about her date with Adam.

"Yes. We're going to Peter's party. How do you like Adam?" Melissa asked sincerely.

"He's really neat, and he has some strong opinions about captains of varsity teams," Jessica said.

"What kind of opinions?" Melissa asked politely.

"He thinks the best member of the team should be the captain." Jessica waited for Melissa's response.

She finally answered. "That seems to make sense."

"Do you think Olivia is the best cheerleader?" Jessica asked.

Again, there was a pause. "I haven't thought about it. She's very good."

After Jessica finished talking to Melissa, she lay back on her bed and thought about being captain of the cheerleaders. She had never been president or captain of anything, and it would be nice to be number one, but how?

The next person Jessica called was Peter. "Your computer dating idea is great," she told him.

"Thanks," he said, a little surprised by her telephone call.

"Adam and I will be at your party," Jessica said.

"Good. How about bringing some chips?" Peter asked. "The guys are helping with the soda and I thought we'd pick up pizzas, too."

"Good idea," Jessica said. Then she switched the subject. "Adam is captain of the swim team."

"I know. He's really good," Peter added.

"They work things differently on the varsity swim team. The captain is the best swimmer," she said and waited for Peter's reaction.

Finally, he said, "I guess every sports team has its way of choosing captains. Maybe the French club picks the person with the best accent!"

"Don't remind me of French!" Jessica snapped.

"Okay, Jessica, Adam is captain and the best swimmer on the team. So what?"

"It's just that he thinks I'm the best athlete of the cheerleaders," Jessica said casually.

"You might be the best *girl* athlete, but personally I think I'm the best guy," Peter said. "So what?"

"Nothing," Jessica said. "Forget it. I'll see you tonight at the Deep River game. 'Bye."

"'Bye," Peter said as he hung up the phone and started rearranging the living room furniture for the party. He was glad he had convinced his mother to go with a friend to the movies and for Chinese food afterward.

The next phone call was from Ken.

"I did it! I asked Melissa to your party!" Ken reported excitedly.

"Super. I knew you could do it," Peter said.

"Did you call Diana and set her up for the blind date?" Ken asked anxiously.

"Not yet, but I'll do it the minute we hang up."

"Do you think you can disguise your voice?" Ken asked nervously. He doubted that he'd ever have the courage to pull a trick on a girl.

"I've got it all planned. I'm going to put some loud, funky music in the background to distract her, and I'm going to make it a very, very short call. Just set a place and time tonight for a date after the game."

"What about your voice?"

Peter cleared his throat and concentrated on lowering the pitch. He spoke slowly as he practiced his opening lines with Ken. "Is Diana Tucker home? Hello, Diana, this is your computer *love* calling to set up a rendezvous."

"Not bad," Ken said, amazed by his friend's vocal talent.

"Thanks." Peter was delighted with his performance. "I'll call her now. 'Bye."

Peter turned up the music, dialed Diana, and waited for Mr. Tucker to put his daughter on the phone. As soon as Diana said hello, Peter went into his prepared speech.

"But what's your name?" Diana pleaded after Peter suggested a blind date at the Pizza Palace after the game.

Peter ignored her question. "I will see you tonight, my Diana. Tonight we will meet and fall in love! Good-bye for now."

When Peter hung up, he burst into laughter. He was sure she'd tell all her friends about her fabulous "blind date." It was the perfect way to get even with her for not giving Hope's message to Mary Ellen.

This should be a great evening, Peter thought, as he moved the dining room table against the wall to make more room for dancing.

CHAPTER

Sean parked his red Fiero in front of Tara's house at four o'clock. He didn't bother to go to the front door. Instead, he tooted his horn twice and Tara came racing out. Zipping up her leather jacket and twisting a red-and-white scarf around her neck, she bounded into Sean's car.

"Hi," Tara said. "This is the dumbest idea!" Sean smiled at her and started the engine.

"Aren't you a little bit curious about us being paired by the computer?" Sean teased. "I am."

"Sean Dubrow, you are not my type. The computer must be wacky," Tara said seriously.

"What is your type?"

"Patrick is my type," Tara answered quickly.

"He wasn't always," Sean said with a big-brother tone in his voice. "I remember a certain teacher named Nick who turned you on, and you've dated almost as much as I have, before Kate, that is. . . ."

"Stop bragging, Sean," Tara said sharply. The handsome cheerleader was beginning to annoy her and they were only five minutes into their date. "Where are we going?"

"To Dopey's. Is that okay?"

Tara nodded as they drove down familiar streets to one of the cheerleaders' favorite hangouts.

"Why do you think we were paired?" Tara asked Sean after a few minutes.

Sean looked at Tara. "Because we're both terrific people. Can't you see us at the Senior Prom? King Sean and Queen Tara . . ." He liked teasing her.

"You are the most conceited guy I know. I thought the Young Mr. Tarenton contest got it out of your system." Tara was delighted that she had an opportunity to give Sean a jab after his dig about her crush on Nick.

At Dopey's, they compared printouts.

"This is amazing," Tara said dramatically. "We both have the same priorities: school, social activities, sports."

"And similar interests," Sean added, reading the sheets carefully. "We could be twins."

"According to Peter and Ken's theory, we should be in love with each other," Tara said. "I don't get it!"

Suddenly Sean started to laugh. "Maybe the problem is too much of a good thing."

Tara joined in the laughter. "Mr. Modesty speaks again!"

Just as they were ordering Cokes, they heard a familiar voice.

"Hi!" Peter called from the entrance of the restaurant.

Sean waved for him to join them.

"So you two *did* get together. How did it go?" Peter asked as he slid into the booth.

"It didn't *go!* We're too alike," Tara said. "I think opposites attract."

"We'll see how the others made out tonight. Are you coming to the party?"

"Sure," Tara said, "but with Patrick."

"And I'm going to give Kate a call." Sean smiled when he said Kate's name. "We're definitely opposites! Peter, who are you bringing to the party?"

"Terri Rogers. We saw each other last night," Peter bragged.

"Good going!" Sean said. "She's great."

"Yes. She's pretty and very bright, too." Peter ordered a Coke and switched the subject. "I've got some shopping to do for the party. Do you want to help?"

"Sure," Sean said. Peter and Sean looked at Tara.

"I'll help clean up after the party, Peter, but I have to go home now. I have to wash my hair and Patrick is picking me up for dinner before the game," Tara said.

"I'll drop you off, Tara," Sean offered. "Then I'll meet you at the discount beverage store, Peter."

"Great!" Peter said.

By five-thirty, Tara was ready to go. Her hair was sparkling clean and blown dry with a new styling brush to make it look even fuller. She was wearing a bulky knit turquoise sweater over black leather pants that clung to her shapely legs. Tabitha, her orange tabby kitten, was curled up on the bed, watching. When Tara finished, she picked up the kitten and hugged her affectionately.

The moment the doorbell rang, Tara dashed to open it. In the past, she would make a date wait for a few minutes before she made her entrance. But ever since she fell in love with Patrick, Tara was always on time.

Patrick greeted her with a hug. Tara loved the feeling of his strong, muscular arms around her.

"I have a surprise for our dinner date," Patrick said as he smiled at Tara. His dark eyes were filled with affection and delight.

Tara felt herself blushing as he took her hand and lead her to the van. Leon, Patrick's dog, was looking out of the window.

"Into the back," Patrick ordered. Leon greeted Tara with a lick and jumped into the rear of the van.

"What's the surprise?" Tara asked happily as she zipped up her jacket.

"Look under the blanket in the back," Patrick said cheerfully. Tara turned around and leaned over the seat to remove the blanket.

"It's a basket."

"A picnic basket," Patrick answered. "I thought we'd drive out to the property I bought and have a picnic supper on the land."

"Oh, Patrick, what a romantic idea!" Tara was thrilled.

"I'll build a small fire to keep us warm and I even packed a candle so that we can eat by candlelight," he said, searching Tara's face for approval.

"We won't have any trouble keeping warm," Tara said, laughing.

"I love you," Patrick said as he leaned over to kiss her.

"I love you, too," Tara answered almost in a whisper.

Melissa and Hope were the first into the girls' locker room. Melissa started to change into her cheerleading uniform. "I got the strangest phone call from Jessica this afternoon," she said.

Hope opened her locker and gave Melissa a questioning look.

"She asked me who I thought was the best cheerleader."

"The best? We're a team and we're all good," Hope said, a little surprised by the question. "I wonder who put the idea into her head."

"I think it was Adam Logan. He's the captain of the varsity swim team and Jessica said the best swimmer is the captain. What do you think, Hope?"

Hope started to undress. The question puzzled her. She had never thought about it. Olivia was voted captain because everyone liked her. "I suppose if someone wanted to judge a cheerleader by athletic ability alone, Jessica *would* be considered the best athlete."

Melissa thought about Hope's answer. Jessica

was always chosen to demonstrate new stunts, and she seemed to perform the acrobatics with unusual ease. "Then, do you think the best athlete should be the captain?"

"Hey, what are you talking about?" Tara asked as she entered the locker room.

"Adam Logan's theory that the best athlete should be the captain of the team," Melissa said. "What do you think?"

Tara shrugged her shoulders. "It makes sense, but what if the best athlete doesn't want to be captain?"

"That's another issue," Hope said as she turned to Jessica, who had just come into the room and was unpacking her knapsack. "What do you think, Jessica?"

"I was impressed with the way the swim team handled their leadership. Adam was really involved in helping his teammates improve their strokes."

When Mary Ellen came into the locker room, the girls were in a heated argument, and Jessica seemed to be initiating it. But the second Olivia entered the room, the girls became quiet, and the subject then changed to their computer dates.

Mary Ellen had never thought about the role of captain of the cheerleaders. Olivia Evans was made captain when Ardith Engborg was coach. Should there be a change? This unrest was bad for the team, and Mary Ellen was worried.

CHAPTER

12

The Tarenton High gymnasium was standing room only. The win last week against St. Cloud created a fever of excitement in the school, and the students were enthusiastically cheering for another victory. Mary Ellen was surprised to see the visitors' section filled with Deep River supporters. A win for Tarenton would put the team in the running for the county championship, and Deep River didn't want to lose their place as contenders. Mary Ellen saw their all-girl cheerleading squad dressed in their blue-and-white uniforms, warming up in the corner of the gym.

Mary Ellen led the Tarenton squad to the benches in front of the home-team section. It was a relief to have everyone present and accounted for.

The five girls and two boys did some stretches and bends and took their places on the bench.

Mrs. Oetjen greeted the students over the loudspeaker. "Please stand for the National Anthem." Everyone stood as the taped music filled the gym. Immediately following the last note, shouts of excitement resounded and the cheerleaders sprang to their feet. They immediately started their welcoming cheer.

Jessica saw Adam sitting in the first row of the grandstand. He was surrounded by varsity swim team members. When Jessica jumped into the air and landed in a split, the entire swim team burst into applause. It was obvious that they were cheering only for Jessica.

Jessica tried not to focus her attention on Adam, but she was drawn to him, and it made her try harder.

Tarenton took an early lead. Olivia called the "After the Basket" cheer.

"And the score goes up another notch,
  Two points! Two points!
  Hey, we're the team to watch!
  We're *BAD!*"

Jessica liked this particular cheer because she stood on Sean's shoulders, then leaped forward and rolled into a front somersault between Olivia and Tara, who were the spotters.

Jessica exploded with energy as she executed the cheer. Adam and his friends went wild, stomping, clapping, and shouting, "Jessica . . . Jessica!"

She felt like a star. During each cheer, Jessica jumped a little higher than everyone else. Her

107

shouts were louder and her smile broader.

The Tarenton Wolves were in excellent form. Ray Elliot, the star center, made one basket after another; Bill Hadley controlled his fouls; and Jeff Daniels delighted the crowd with his fancy dribbling and passing.

The Tarenton cheerleaders followed each play with a cheer. During a name cheer for Bill Hadley, Jessica leaped so high that she lost her balance for a second and landed in front of Olivia, blocking the captain's leap. Jessica threw her arms up in the classic winner's position, and Olivia wobbled, almost falling.

"Watch out!" Olivia snapped angrily at Jessica. "What's the matter with you?"

"She brought her own cheering section," Tara said as she steadied Olivia by holding her arm.

"Sorry," Jessica said instantly.

Mary Ellen immediately walked over to Olivia. "Are you all right?"

Olivia shook herself for a moment. "Fine. I'm fine."

Mary Ellen turned to Jessica. Her face was clouded with disapproval. "This isn't like you, Jessica. You've been upstaging everyone all evening. Calm down."

Jessica nodded. She didn't want to upset anyone. She looked over at Adam and saw him smiling and waving to her. She waved back and quickly forgot about Mary Ellen's remark.

During halftime, Tarenton was beating Deep River by sixteen points.

"Can we do 'The Bird' cheer?" Jessica asked Mary Ellen.

Mary Ellen hesitated before she agreed to use the new cheer. Olivia frowned when she heard Mary Ellen call for it.

"Don't try anything fancy," Mary Ellen warned. "This is a dangerous stunt and I don't want an accident!"

Jessica nodded and took her position at the end of the line for the cheer. Sean studied her carefully and did a few knee bends to prepare for the leap. The spotters quickly checked out the mounting and lift position. Melissa gave out the red-and-white pompons to Hope and Peter and kept one for herself. Since this was a line cheer and not partnered, Melissa was included. Olivia and Tara spotted, so their hands were free.

The cheerleaders formed a line with Sean turned toward Jessica on the opposite end. When the positions for the cheer were set, Jessica heard Adam's voice bellowing out from the crowd.

She looked into the audience and saw Adam standing with both his hands raised as if giving a benediction. "Quiet! Quiet everyone! This is a very difficult stunt!"

The spectators quieted down a little and Jessica was embarrassed. No one ever announced a cheer as "a very difficult stunt" to the audience. The whole idea of cheerleading was not to make it look difficult, but she didn't have time to stop and think.

Olivia called the cheer, and on the count of three, the squad started chanting. Every eye in the room was watching them.

"We've scored.
We've won.
We're number one.
Tarenton Wolves . . . let's fly!"

Jessica started her run toward Sean. She leaped into his arms during the shouts of "let's fly!" and for a moment, she was a bird soaring through the air.

The audience burst into frantic applause as the cheer ended and Jessica stepped forward. She could hear Adam's shouts of "bravo" above the noise.

Sean patted her on the shoulder. "Good job," he said, but no one else on the squad reacted to her performance.

During the second half of the Deep River game, the cheerleaders ignored Jessica, as she continued to play to Adam and his friends.

Tarenton beat Deep River by a good margin, twenty points, and the students cheered ecstatically, but there was tension in the girls' locker room.

Tara passed Jessica and said, "Looks like you have your own fan club."

Jessica laughed and pulled her heavy sweater over her head.

Olivia took the opportunity to discuss the subject. "I think it would be a good idea," she said seriously, "if your friend was less enthusiastic for a particular cheerleader and more involved with the game."

Jessica wanted to reply, "You're just jealous," but she knew there was truth in what Olivia was saying.

"I'll mention it," Jessica said, turning away from the captain and continuing to undress.

"Are you taking him to Peter's party?" Tara asked.

Jessica nodded and asked, "Are you going with Sean?"

Tara started to laugh. "You must be kidding. Sean and I are like brother and sister. He's taking Kate and I'll be with Patrick," she said as she toyed with the ring on her finger. "I told Peter it was a waste pairing me with anyone."

Melissa was wrapped in a beach towel when she passed Tara. "I'm going with Ken." She had a dreamy smile on her face.

"She looks happy," Olivia said to Tara, avoiding Jessica.

After showering, Jessica dressed in her skin-tight, navy blue cords and lush sky-blue angora sweater. She brushed her hair vigorously and pulled one side back with a large rhinestone clip. As she put on a light coral lip gloss, she smiled at her reflection in the mirror. Adam will like this outfit, she thought as she walked toward the exit.

"Jessica, can I speak with you?" Mary Ellen called from her office.

"Sure," Jessica said as she turned and smiled at the coach. Mary Ellen didn't return the smile.

"Please close the door before you sit down," Mary Ellen said.

Jessica's expression became serious as she followed the coach's orders. She sat across from Mary Ellen and waited.

"What happened to you tonight?" Mary Ellen asked.

Jessica looked puzzled, but she didn't answer.

"You were upstaging Olivia," Mary Ellen continued.

"Oh, that. It was an accident. Everyone made such a big deal out of it," Jessica said as she played with her school ring nervously.

Mary Ellen took a deep breath before she went on. She found it difficult to confront a cheerleader, especially one who was a friend. They had become close only a few months ago when Jessica was failing French, and Mary Ellen had taken the role of big sister. But now things were changed. Mary Ellen was the coach, and she had to get to the bottom of the problem.

"Jessica, you were not performing like a member of the team," Mary Ellen stated.

"Maybe I'm just a better cheerleader! I can't be expected not to jump or kick my highest!" Jessica said defensively.

"The purpose of a cheerleading team is to work as a team. This isn't a play, where there are stars and supporting players," Mary Ellen said angrily.

"I understand what you're saying, but I've been thinking about the team, and I wonder if we're really doing the best we can. Some of the squad members don't seem able to perform as well as others," Jessica said, trying to hide her discomfort.

"Everyone doesn't have the same talents.

You happen to be the best athlete, but the others are excellent cheerleaders," Mary Ellen said.

"On the swim team the best swimmer is the captain. That way he can encourage the others to excel," Jessica explained.

Mary Ellen looked at Jessica and smiled. "I get it now, Jessica. You want to be captain."

It was a difficult moment and Jessica hesitated before she answered. "Adam Logan thinks it would be good for the team."

Mary Ellen became angry. "I don't care what Adam Logan thinks! Judging from the way he and his friends were disrupting the cheers with their applause, he doesn't have good judgment."

"He was just trying to be supportive," Jessica said defensively.

"Supportive of you alone, Jessica, not the basketball team or the cheerleaders," Mary Ellen continued, her anger growing.

Jessica backed down. "I know, and I'm sorry. I'll speak to him tonight."

Mary Ellen was glad that Jessica realized how rude the swim team captain had been at the Deep River game. "I'd appreciate that, Jessica. Now about being captain. I'll think about what you've said."

"Thanks, Mary Ellen."

"You can go now," the coach said, adding, "and have fun at Peter's party!"

"I will," Jessica said and smiled.

CHAPTER

13

Peter was excited about the party, but he had mixed emotions about his date with Terri.

Ken was standing outside the locker room, pacing nervously, when Peter opened the door. "Hi," Peter said, greeting him with a big welcoming smile.

"Oh, hi, Peter," Ken said anxiously. He started flipping his car keys from hand to hand. "I'm waiting for Melissa."

Peter caught the keys between flips and tossed them high into the air. "Don't be so uptight, Ken. Melissa's a great kid, and I guarantee you'll like each other."

"I like her already, but will she like *me?*" Ken questioned shyly.

Peter gave the thumbs-up sign. "You know it!"

"We had a terrific phone conversation, but a

date isn't as easy," Ken admitted to his project partner.

"You'll do great," Peter said, tossing the keys back to Ken. "Listen, I've got to get to the house before the guests arrive." Peter strutted down the hall and into the gymnasium, where he was meeting Terri.

Terri was standing with Tara and Patrick at the far end of the room. As he walked toward them, he was startled by the beauty of the two girls. Tara's red hair and dazzling smile illuminated the room, and Terri's delicate blonde appearance balanced the picture. Peter's stomach started to flutter as he approached the trio.

The girls continued to talk as Peter joined the group. "Do you need a lift or do you have your car?" Patrick asked Peter without interrupting the girls' conversation.

"Thanks, but I have the MG. I'll meet you at the apartment," Peter said. The boys waited patiently for the girls to finish.

Peter cleared his throat and tried to speak with perfect diction. "We have to get going, Terri."

Terri said a quick good-bye to Tara. "I'll see you at Peter's."

Peter and Terri walked quickly to the parking lot. "I didn't know you knew Tara," Peter finally said after a long pause.

"We took some classes together," Terri said.

"What are your plans after graduation?" Peter asked as he helped Terri into the car.

She didn't answer until he was seated next to

her. "I've really been struggling with that question."

Peter decided not to rush her into an answer by grilling her further.

"I've applied to the Rhode Island School of Design as an art major, and to Yale as a theater major."

"But I thought you weren't interested in acting," Peter asked, slightly confused.

"I'm interested in set design, and it falls under theater, but it might be too narrow a major. I've also applied to State. They have a very good applied art and art history department."

Terri continued her monologue about the differences in college art programs. By the time Peter parked the car in front of his apartment, he felt a little more comfortable. He didn't mind that Terri hadn't asked him about his plans, because the pressure was off him to contribute sparkling conversation. In minutes, they were at his front door.

Ken had helped Peter decorate the living room with old computer printouts, and they had hung old floppy disks on strings from the dining room fixture. Across the wall, behind the couch, Ken had printed a giant sign that read, WELCOME COMPUTER DATES. Peter had pushed the dining room table against the wall, covered the table with more printouts, and put out cans of soft drinks and bowls of pretzels and chips.

As soon as Peter entered the apartment, he started the music. "I've got to do a few things before everyone arrives," he said.

"Where should I put my coat?" Terri looked around the room.

"Just throw it on the bed in my room," Peter said just as the doorbell rang. "They're here already!"

Terri could hear the excitement in Peter's voice. "I'll get it," she said.

"Thanks," Peter said as he dashed into the kitchen and started for the refrigerator. He dumped ice cubes into a mixing bowl as the voices of his friends filled the apartment.

By the time he entered the living room, Hope and her date, Matt Nikolias, were putting a tape in the tape machine, and Melissa and Olivia were taking their coats into the bedroom, leaving Ken and Scott to talk about the basketball game.

Terri spied Matt and immediately turned her attention to the sensitive-looking musician. "You're in the orchestra, aren't you?" she said, smiling sweetly.

"Cello," Matt said, obviously enjoying her attention.

"I've studied the viola," Terri said intently.

"Why aren't you in the orchestra?" he asked, ignoring Hope, who had returned from the bedroom.

"I'm a perfectionist, and honestly, I wasn't good enough. I feel my real talent is in the visual arts," Terri said candidly.

"I'm a perfectionist, too," Matt said. His deep-set eyes were studying Terri's delicate features.

Hope looked at the pair, deep in conversation, and decided not to interrupt them. She was delighted when the doorbell rang and she could help welcome the guests.

The room filled up quickly. Jessica and Adam were the first to slow dance to a new Lionel Richie release. Patrick and Tara swayed to the beat, too. Hope, Peter, and Scott were rehashing the basketball and football season.

Olivia gently pulled Scott away from the group and asked, "How about a dance?" She loved the smooth, slow music.

"Sure," Scott said uneasily. "But I've got to warn you, I'm better at disco."

"That's okay," Olivia said, steering him to the area near the speakers where the other couples were dancing.

Olivia felt his muscular arms around her, and he began to search for the beat. It took him a while to find the rhythm and lead her into a simple step.

They danced in silence, and Olivia realized she wasn't enjoying being in Scott's arms. The special feeling was missing. It was similar to their conversations — they had things in common, but they just didn't work as a couple. The special "it" that Olivia felt with Walt and Duffy wasn't there.

When the music stopped, Olivia and Scott walked back to the group. Scott immediately started talking to Melissa, Peter, and Hope about the basketball game.

Ken switched the subject to future uses for their computer program. Melissa finally decided to ask Ken to dance. It was a lovely slow oldie, and they felt comfortable in each other's arms. The last to arrive were Kate and Sean.

Kate's curly hair was flying and her cheeks were rosy. Her eyes looked extra large behind her wire-framed glasses. Sean's arm was around her protectively.

Hope bent over and whispered to Olivia. "Looks like a little competition from a computer date has brought those two closer."

Olivia watched the affectionate couple. "Opposites *can* attract."

Terri and Matt started to dance while Peter brought out more sodas. Ken whispered to him from the doorway, "It looks like Matt Nikolias is making a play for your date. Do you want me to say something?"

Peter looked up at the pair dancing on the far side of the room and smiled. "No. It's okay."

"But Terri Rogers was *your* perfect match, and she sure is a beauty!"

"But beauty isn't everything," Peter said philosophically.

Sean reached over for a soda and overheard the tail end of the conversation. "Is that the ladies' man, Peter Rayman, saying that 'beauty isn't everything'? Now I've heard it all."

Peter started to laugh. "I must be changing."

Sean continued. "You were looking for the perfect date, and Terri Rogers certainly seems like it. Bright, beautiful, and — "

"And flirtatious," Ken added, watching the pair chatter and dance.

"And we weren't comfortable together. It

may have looked like a match, but it didn't work out that way. To have a perfect date you have to be comfortable," Peter said.

"All that work for nothing," Sean said. "Look, I was matched with Tara, and Kate is the one for me." He took two cans of soda and walked over to Kate, who was talking to Hope.

"Melissa worked for me," Ken said proudly.

"But you *fixed* the computer," Peter reminded his friend.

Ken blushed.

"That reminds me," Peter continued. He held up his arms to quiet the room, and signaled for Olivia to turn down the music.

"Remember Diana?" Peter said.

A loud "boo" came from Sean. Everyone laughed.

"Remember how we all said we wished we could get even with her for not giving Mary Ellen the message from Hope?" he continued.

"Really!" Hope said. "I've never been so angry in my life!"

"Ken and I thought of a way to make her get the message that she shouldn't mess with the cheerleaders," Peter said proudly.

"How?" Hope asked.

Ken explained to the group how he had set up a fictitious date for Diana, using the computer. Everyone started applauding.

"I love it," Hope said. "She's going to think she has a date with Mr. Perfect, and no one will show up!"

"She's probably waiting at the Pizza Palace right now. I wish I could see it," Olivia said.

Peter smiled. "You can," he said. The room became quiet. "I thought we'd pick up some pizzas for the party."

"Terrific idea! We can see Diana suffer first-hand," Jessica said bitterly. "When I was having trouble with French, she started that awful rumor that I was off the team."

"I remember," Melissa said. "And when we were competing for the alternate cheerleader slot, Diana did everything possible to put me down. She was a real sore loser."

Peter picked up an empty paper cup and started passing it around the room. "If everyone puts in two dollars, we should have enough for two large special pizzas."

"Who gets to pick up the pies at the Pizza Palace?" Hope asked anxiously. "I *have* to be there!"

"Agreed," Peter said. "We need three more volunteers."

All the cheerleaders in the room raised their hands and started shouting.

Peter looked around the room and wished all the cheerleaders could go. He turned to Ken. "You choose," he said.

Ken had no problem choosing Hope, Olivia, Peter, and Sean. Peter collected the money, and in minutes the four had their coats on and were gone.

When they had left, the remaining guests started talking about cheerleading. Adam cornered Tara and Melissa while Jessica was clearing space on the table for the pizzas.

"Wasn't Jessica terrific today doing that flying

cheer? She looked like a bird," he said proudly. Tara and Melissa listened politely.

"I wish I had had a camera! She's fantastic," he continued bragging. Ken brought over a glass of soda for Melissa and stood behind her listening to Adam.

"She's the best! Don't you agree?" Adam said to Ken.

"They're all great cheerleaders," Ken said. "I think he's a little starstruck with Jessica," he said to the girls. They smiled.

"She *is* the best acrobat," Melissa admitted. "I wish I could do some of the stunts she can do."

Tara just shrugged her shoulders. "Cheerleading isn't just doing stunts."

Jessica paid attention to the conversation even though her back was to the group. She heard Adam's voice above the others.

"1 think Jessica should be the captain," he said clearly.

Jessica felt as though someone had punched her in the stomach.

No one made a comment as Adam continued. "She'd be a great inspiration to everyone. I firmly believe that the best should be the leader."

Jessica spun around and faced Adam. Rage shook her body. "How dare you suggest to the others that I replace Olivia! She's the captain *and* my friend!"

Adam looked surprised as he tried to defend himself against the angry cheerleader. "But you're number one . . . the best!"

122

"No, I'm one of seven. No one is number one and you have no right talking about me to my friends. Cheerleading is none of your business."

Adam held his hands up in the position of surrender. "Okay, I'm sorry. Forget it, ladies," he said, bowing slightly and giving a charming half smile to them.

"Let's dance," Ken said to Melissa, trying to break up the uncomfortable situation.

"Let's clean up," Jessica said to Tara, "before the others come back with the pizzas." She was angry at Adam and she wanted to get away from him to sort out her thoughts.

In the kitchen, Tara said, "That was some scene."

"I'm sorry, Tara," Jessica said seriously. "I was very embarrassed."

Tara comforted her friend. "Forget it! Adam's crazy about you and he just got carried away. Do you like him?"

"I don't know anymore. I did, but that was yesterday."

Pres picked up Mary Ellen after the game. "Hungry?" Pres asked.

Mary Ellen nodded. "Being the coach makes you almost as hungry as being a cheerleader."

Pres gave his wife a kiss on the cheek before he started the car. "You were the most beautiful cheerleader Tarenton High ever had."

Pres could always make Mary Ellen blush. "And you were the most hungry," she replied. "Once you ate four slices of pizza!"

"Can't do that anymore or I'll get middle-age

spread," he teased as he patted his stomach. "But let's stop at the Pizza Palace, anyway!"

"Fine."

They drove in silence for a few blocks. Pres looked over at his beautiful young wife. "Penny for your thoughts."

Mary Ellen frowned. "Jessica. She thinks she wants to be captain of the team."

"Why? Olivia is captain," Pres said.

"I think her computer date, Adam Logan, put the idea into her head. He's a very aggressive person and the captain of the varsity swim team."

"Oh, an instigator, eh?" Pres said. "What does Jessica say?"

"It's not exactly what she says, but what she's doing. Tonight she was upstaging Olivia and almost caused an accident."

"That's not good," Pres agreed.

"As far as words go, she's been hinting. What do you think I should do about it? There's been a lot of gossip going on."

Pres thought for a while. Finally he asked, "Is Olivia a good captain?"

"Yes. There's no reason to replace her, but I have to put an end to the gossip and bickering. I don't know what to do." Mary Ellen felt Pres's hand reach for hers and give her an affectionate squeeze.

"You'll work it out. I have faith in you," he said sincerely.

They drove in silence to the Pizza Palace. The parking lot in front was filled with cars, so they parked behind the restaurant.

"Looks like the immediate world is here," Pres said as he opened the car door for Mary Ellen.

"I don't recognize any of the cars!" Mary Ellen said glancing around the parking lot. "I wonder who's inside?"

CHAPTER

Hope, Olivia, and Peter crammed into Sean's car. Sean switched on the radio and turned up the volume. Peter reached over from the back to turn it down as Sean started the car.

"What do you think about your computer dates?" Peter asked enthusiastically.

Olivia was sitting next to Sean. She turned and looked seriously at Peter. "It was a clever idea, Peter. Was it yours or Ken's?"

"My idea and his execution," Peter bragged.

"You should both get A's," Hope said.

"It would probably be your first," Sean teased.

Peter laughed. "Okay, hot shot, I'm interested in your computer dates. Did they work?"

"Are you kidding?" Sean asked. "Tara and me, we're like brother and sister."

"She's beautiful," Peter said, waiting to hear

Sean's reaction. "You'd make one good-looking couple."

"Thanks, but my heart belongs to Kate. She's different, and I find that very exciting. Plus, in case you forgot, Tara and Patrick are engaged."

Hope was deep in thought. "I think Sean stumbled on the problem. I had the same feelings about Matt. Even though we have a lot in common, I feel much closer to Tony Pell."

"Yes. I noticed that you didn't seem to be upset when he danced with Terri," Sean suggested.

Peter shrugged his shoulders and gave a sheepish look at the driver. "We didn't take," he admitted.

"What does that mean?" Olivia asked.

"I can't put my finger on it, but Terri and I just didn't hit it off," Peter answered.

Hope's face lit up. Perhaps the 'birds of a feather, flock together' theory creates friends and *not* couples."

"Could be," Olivia said. "Scott's a nice guy, and even though we have some things in common, there's no spark!"

"What do you think of Jessica and Adam Logan?" Hope asked the group. For a moment, there was silence.

Peter spoke first, "Not much!"

"He's a troublemaker," Sean said.

"Sometimes I think *he* wants to be captain of the cheerleaders," Peter said. He looked at Olivia and noticed that she seemed uncomfortable. "Don't worry, Olivia, that hunk is all wet!"

Everyone laughed at Peter's pun. "I hope Jessica drops him," he said.

Olivia still looked thoughtful as the car pulled up in front of the Pizza Palace. "We'll have to pull around in the back to park," Sean said as he maneuvered the car to an empty parking space.

"Isn't that Mary Ellen and Pres's car?" Olivia said. She pointed to the car with the Tarenton Community College sticker.

"Could be," Sean said.

Everyone jumped out of the car and started for the restaurant.

"I can just see Diana, sitting all alone in a booth, looking out of the window forlornly," Peter said dramatically.

"I hope you're right," Hope said as they walked up the path to the front door. "I hope she's alone and miserable."

"Now, now, Hope," Sean said calmly, "we don't want her in tears."

"Diana has probably never been stood up in her whole life," Olivia said. "It'll be good for her soul!"

Peter held the door open for the girls. "Let's take a look."

As soon as they went up the steps into the Pizza Palace, they got into a line for outgoing orders.

"Peter! Hope!" Mary Ellen exclaimed with surprise. "What are you guys doing here?"

"Picking up pizzas for the party," Peter said. "Anyone else here from school?"

Pres extended his hand to Sean and Peter and greeted them. "Looks like the entire Deep River basketball team is here."

"Losers get hungry, too," Sean added as he craned his neck to get a better look at the circle of boys sitting around two tables that were pushed together.

Suddenly Olivia shouted, "Do you see who I see?" She pointed to the far end of the table.

"Oh, no!" Peter said.

"I can't believe that girl," Hope said as she shook her head.

Mary Ellen and Pres turned around to face the table. "It's just Diana Tucker," Mary Ellen said, a little confused by the cheerleaders' sudden attention to the Deep River group.

Sean suddenly ducked his head and turned away. "She was supposed to be alone."

"And miserable," Hope said.

"Instead, she has the whole Deep River team paying court to her," Olivia said and sighed.

"Let's order the pizzas and get out of here," Peter said nervously. "I'd rather she didn't see me. She just might put two and two together and set the Deep River team on me."

Hope started to giggle and couldn't stop.

"It's not funny," Peter said as he handed the money to her. "Here, you do the ordering and I'll wait in the car."

When Peter fled, Olivia explained the situation about Diana and the blind date to Mary Ellen and Pres. In a few minutes, everyone was laughing.

"But Diana got the last laugh," Mary Ellen said as she looked over at the pretty girl surrounded by the rival team.

Diana noticed the coach, then gave a big wave and flashed a full smile.

"She doesn't seem angry," Pres said to the cheerleaders. "If it happened to me, I'd be out for blood."

"Diana isn't like other people. She can turn anything around to her own advantage," Olivia said. "The truth is, she got us, we didn't get her!"

Mary Ellen and Pres took a booth. Hope, Olivia, and Sean waited near the cashier for the pizzas. They could see Diana's table, but they decided to turn their backs to her.

Hope said, "Ken and Peter did have a good plan. Too bad it didn't work!"

They brought the pizzas back to the party and told the Diana story to everyone. The entire group broke up into laughter.

After they finished eating, Peter turned down the lights and put on soft dance music. Ken asked Melissa to dance. She cuddled into his arms and rested her head on his chest.

"I'm glad we were paired," Melissa said, looking up into his eyes.

"I have to tell you something," Ken said shyly.

Melissa continued to gaze into his eyes as he spoke.

"I picked you for my date," Ken said.

"Yes, I understand how it worked. You put my name into your computer."

"No, I picked you and then made you come out as my date," he admitted. "I've felt funny about not telling you the truth. You were never really a part of the general questionnaire pool."

Melissa looked puzzled. "How did you do it?"

"I saw you at cheerleading practice, and I wanted to date you," Ken said as they slow danced.

"Why didn't you just call me?" Melissa asked.

"I . . . I was afraid you wouldn't go out with me. Then I got the idea of making you my computer date. That way, I was sure you'd go out with me at least once. Are you angry?"

Melissa looked at the intense young man. A slow smile filled her face. "I'm flattered."

"You are?"

"Sure. You *wanted* to date me. We weren't a computer match, and I think that's great!"

"You do?"

"Yes, I do," Melissa said as she snuggled closer and enjoyed the feeling of his arms around her.

Patrick placed a kiss on Tara's neck as they danced. She looked up into his eyes. "I love you," she said.

Sean talked to Kate about the Diana set-up as they danced. Kate didn't appreciate the joke.

"Just because she does rotten things doesn't mean you have to stoop to her level," Kate said. "What if she hadn't connected with the Deep River players?"

"But she did . . . unfortunately. Kate, let's forget it and enjoy the party," Sean said as he pulled her closer to him.

Hope and Matt left early. When they were saying good-night, Hope noticed that Matt lingered to speak privately with Terri while she was getting her coat from the bedroom.

They talked about the orchestra on the way home, and Hope said good-night in the car when they reached her house.

"You don't have to get out," she said politely. "Peter and Ken had a really interesting idea, but I don't think computer dating works."

Matt looked a little uncomfortable.

"I'll see you at music class," Hope said as she walked away.

When she was undressing, her phone rang. Hope caught it on the first ring so that she wouldn't wake her family. It was Olivia.

"What did you think?" Olivia asked.

"Matt isn't for me. He's nice, but there's no chemistry, like with me and Tony."

"Same with me and Scott," Olivia said. "We hardly spoke in the car going home."

"What do you think about Jessica and Adam Logan?" Hope asked.

Olivia hesitated before she answered. "I've heard about Adam's theory — the best athlete should be captain," Olivia said.

"Don't listen to him. He has a big mouth," Hope said, trying to put Olivia at ease. "You're the best captain we could have."

"Thanks for your vote of confidence, but the truth is, maybe he's right!"

"No! Olivia, stop talking like that. You're the best!" Hope stated emphatically.

"Thanks, Hope. Got to go. I just wanted to hear how things went with Matt."

"They went nowhere," Hope answered, and she heard Olivia laugh, too.

Tara and Patrick dropped Terri off at her home in Fable Point. Terri asked questions about Matt during the drive. After she was dropped off, Patrick said, "So much for Peter's perfect date." He put his arms around Tara and kissed her.

Jessica was still angry at Adam when they arrived at her house. Adam could sense it, so he confined his conversation to neutral subjects. She let him kiss her good-night on the cheek when they got to the door, but when he asked about seeing her again, Jessica said, "I can't make any plans now."

Ken and Melissa helped Peter clean up the apartment. "Great party," Ken said enthusiastically as he filled a plastic bag with trash.

Melissa was putting bottles in the refrigerator.

"It was okay, but I'm a little disappointed," Peter admitted. He was pushing the table back into its original position. "I was hoping I'd fall in love with the perfect date tonight."

Melissa turned around and said, "You have a Cinderella complex!"

"A what?" Peter asked.

"You wanted the perfect girl to come to your

party, and you'd be Prince Charming, and the two of you would live happily ever after."

Peter started to laugh. "That's ridiculous! Girls wait for a Prince Charming to carry them off on a white horse."

"And guys wait for Cinderella wearing a glass slipper," Melissa said.

Ken chuckled, "I think she's got something there, Peter."

Peter sighed. "Terri Rogers is not my Cinderella."

CHAPTER

Cheerleading practice was held after school on Monday. One by one, the squad entered the gym and started individual warm-ups.

Mary Ellen entered the gym and called to the group. "I'd like to talk to everyone before we start our practice." She signaled for them to come forward and sit in a semicircle. Olivia avoided eye contact with her teammates and sat next to Mary Ellen.

Mary Ellen's expression was serious. "I have a very difficult subject to discuss with you. Olivia and I have spoken confidentially about it."

The gym was still, and every eye was on Mary Ellen. Olivia was sure that her teammates could hear her heart pounding.

Mary Ellen continued. "Olivia has done an excellent job as your captain, but if the team feels that there should be another election, Olivia said she would understand."

Olivia stared at the grains of wood in the floor. She could feel her teammates' stares.

"Olivia wants to do what is best for the team," Mary Ellen said. "What do you think?"

The team was stunned. No one spoke. Instead, they looked at each other.

Suddenly, Jessica stood up and faced the group. "No," she said resolutely. "I don't think there should be another election. It's all my fault because Adam pushed me into thinking that I should be captain. But the truth is, I'm happy just being on the team. I don't need a title. Maybe Adam does, but he's not me. In fact, we're not even dating, and he can put his name back into Ken's computer."

There was a burst of applause.

"I think Olivia is the best captain we could have. She cares about the team and she's a good leader, and I want her to be *my* captain."

"Right on," Sean shouted.

"A cheer for Olivia!" Jessica said as she ran into the center of the gym. Her teammates followed her lead and made a giant circle. Hope grabbed Olivia's hand and led her into the center of the circle.

"Give me an 'O'!" Jessica shouted.

The cheerleaders repeated the letter as they jumped into an open stance with arms out to the side.

"An 'L'!"

As they repeated the letter L, they clapped their hands overhead. Olivia stood beaming in the center of the circle.

Jessica spelled out the remaining letters of

Olivia's name and the cheerleaders repeated each letter with the rehearsed movement. After the "A," Jessica shouted, "She's the best!"

"No," said Olivia. "I'm not the best. *We're* the best. And we're getting better all the time!"

Do you remember when Olivia, Hope, Jessica, Sean, Peter, and Tara became cheerleaders? If not, find out how it all began! Read Cheerleaders #20, STARTING OVER.

Don't miss any exciting adventures of the popular Cheerleaders of Tarenton High!

Complete series available wherever you buy books.